FLIRT LIKE A CHAMP

WILLOW SANDERS

EDITED BY **BRIGGS CONSULTING, LLC**

PROOFREAD BY **CRYSTAL GRIZZARD BURNETTE**

COVER DESIGN BY **WILLOW SANDERS**

DEDICATION

To every single reader out there who chooses to love, light, and support, over negativity and vitriol. Keep burning bright.

PROLOGUE

Harlow

This week on the Bear and Raven Show, we're doing things a bit differently. One of our partners, The Flirt Files, had asked us to partner with them on their special fiftieth episode, where they discussed the art of the flirt. Raven and I were so entertained by Farrah and Freddie's show that we asked to partner with them for a giveaway. Four days, three nights, at the Aria Resort and Casino, for two.

Do you need help in the flirt department? Give us a call, and you could spend the 4th of July Holiday in Las Vegas.

Bear and Raven were my favorites. They'd been in Chicago for about a year, and I listened to them religiously. Farrah and Freddie were new to the syndicate as well. I listened to them with less frequency, but I thought the vacation would be great for my sister and I to take together. A perfect excuse to let our hair down and have an incredible girls' weekend.

What I didn't know is just how gloriously bad I was at flirting, and how that deficiency would turn into the craziest four days of my life.

CHAPTER 1

CASH 

t's not easy being the older brother of a celebrity. If that's
even what my brother was. He swam in the Olympics. People
knew who he was. I guess that made him famous. Or,
infamous. It depended on what side of the coin you looked at.
Beckett Murray, swimming wonderkid, royal fuckup. Caught
with his pants down—literally—at the Rio Games.

It was all behind him now, of course. My little brother was all
grown up. An actual responsible adult, living some fantastic life in
San Diego with a mortgage and a famous-in-her-own-right
girlfriend, Lane.

There were four of us Murray kids. Me, as the oldest, then
Beckett, Presley, and Harris. All four of us swam. My mom put us
all in classes after Beckett nearly drowned. From what I can
remember of my years in swimming, I was more interested in
sneaking peeks in the girl's locker room than actually being good
at any specific stroke. Unless you count the solo kind. Molly
Templeton's nipples, poking through her nearly see-thru lycra
suit, got me every time.

Beckett, of course, was the phenom. Presley always lived in
Beckett's shadow. Never *quite* good enough for the Olympic
team, but still got a full ride to Stanford. Those who can't do,

teach. Isn't that how the saying went? And that's what we planned to celebrate. It was, in fact, the impetus to how I found myself in Las Vegas over the 4th of July. Presley got himself some big deal fucking job at the University of Texas. He'd oversee the men and women's swim teams. We decided to all come to Vegas as a last hurrah before he moved to Texas.

"I know it's just for the weekend," Harris' arms draped around the necks of me and Presley. "But I'm so happy to see you two. I never see either of you anymore."

Harris lived with Beckett. Since graduating, he'd started his own little empire teaching kids how not to be afraid of the ocean. From what Beckett told me, Harris discovered quite the successful niche. The next step, according to Beckett, was for Harris to take that success and rent a place of his own. Especially because he and Lane now lived together, and Harris definitely impeded upon their ability to have crazy hang from the rafters sex.

"There are oceans in Texas." Beckett laughed and pointed toward Presley. "You could always try to diversify your business."

"Or Atlantic City." Presley held up his hands in a "not it," fashion, tossing his head in my direction. "Sure, there's probably a never-ending presence of sharks off the Atlantic coast, but hey, all the more reason to teach kids what to do when you see a fin."

I hated Atlantic City. The manufactured glitz and glamor of whatever decade the boardwalk was still relevant had descended into a shithole of run-down and abandoned hotels. Unfortunately, as the casinos gasped for air to harken back to the glory days, the poker pots were always triple what they were in Las Vegas.

After college, while struggling to figure out exactly *what* I wanted to do with my life, I stumbled into online poker. From online poker, I found the tournament circuit and began playing. They don't tell dumb kids who think they're hot shit, to turn down people who approach you and offer you money to "stake" you in a tournament. Staking was a form of floating an entrant the money it cost to join, for a split of the winnings on the back end. It had been a rookie mistake. One that cost me years of winnings. The interest in Texas Hold 'Em tournaments had been cooling for a few years now, except in Atlantic City. Which was where I'd lived for a few years.

"Beck, get your damn nose out of your phone. I'm sure Lane can survive forty-eight hours without you." I tossed a peanut in his direction, signaling to our waitress for another round.

"It's actually ESPN, you goon." Beckett used the back of his phone case to bat away the line drive peanut. "They want Presley and me to do an interview together."

Beckett currently provided color commentary and expertise to practically every swimming competition known to man. Whether it was the Summer Olympics, the trials, the NCAA swimming finals—the cameras couldn't get enough of him.

"The two of us?" Presley perked up. "Why?"

"Two Murray brothers, a swimming empire makes." Harris laughed. "There seems to be a whole lot of hooting and hollering over at that poker table. I'm going to check it out."

I looked toward where Harris had sauntered off to. We were staying at the Aria. It had a reputation for some fantastic table games, and tonight certainly wasn't any different. A huge crowd gathered around a single table. Every so often, a cacophony of gasps, cheers, and groans echoed across the casino.

The table was down to two people playing that hand. That was far from uncommon in a poker room. However, it was the woman at the table, who looked like she'd just kissed Auntie Em goodbye in Kansas and headed off in the direction of the City of Sin, that had my feet moving toward where she played.

Her nondescript brown hair hung loosely in a braid. The woman wore practically no makeup other than a berry-colored flush clear down to her chest. She wore unicorns on her fingernails that harkened back to the Lisa Frank days of the mid-nineties. It was her t-shirt, however, that stole my attention. Although she had breasts for days, that actually wasn't what drew me to her chest. It was the "Big Fun" broadcast across that expanse which had me chuckling. Clearly eighties pop-culture was her jam. The shirt was a reference to a cult classic named *Heathers.* There was no way she could be old enough to have been around during the *Heathers* craze. I was thirty-seven and even I had been pretty young when that movie came out.

"I'm all in." She pushed all of her chips into the center.

She had a good hand. I could tell even passively watching her. The flush got deeper the moment she shoved her chips into the pile. The greaseball with the potbelly playing across from her asked the dealer what her all in was. As the dealer provided the figure, she checked her cards again. Rookie mistake. If the asshole sitting across from her had any skill, he'd know just by that one action she had a good hand. If I had to guess, she had pocket royalty. There was an Ace and a Jack on the table, and given how red her cheeks were, a royal flush wasn't out of the question.

"Fold." The guy across from her called, and the entire pot went to her.

With glee, she gathered all her chips, tossed a $20 chip toward the dealer, and left the table.

CHAPTER 2

Harlow

My sister got a divorce. That was why we were in Vegas. Well, that and I'd won a contest on the *Bear and Raven Morning Show*, demonstrating for them exactly how bad I was at being flirtatious. Thanks to my god-awful skills at attempting to be attractive, we found ourselves staying at the super swanky Aria resort for the 4th of July holiday.

Lennox and I flew out of Chicago at nine in the morning. Given the two-hour time difference between Chicago and Vegas, we arrived mid-morning and couldn't check into our rooms until after three. Mistake on our part. The other mistake? Grabbing our bathing suits from our suitcases and heading out to the pool where the drinks never stopped coming. Lennox barely made it through dinner and calling our mom to check in on her son, before passing out, ass up, in our hotel room.

Left to my own devices, I'd somehow graduated from video poker to finding a set of balls large enough to sit me down at a live poker table. What possessed me to try my hand with big dogs? I had no clue. And, by big dogs, I meant the $5 tables.

"That was impressive."

Some guy took a seat next to me at the bar sometime later. My winnings came to almost a thousand dollars. For a few hands of poker!

"Thanks."

The guy who sat next to me wasn't unattractive, mind you. Hair more sable than chestnut, a self-assured smile that showed off straight, brilliantly white teeth, and beautiful manicured hands. His hands! I don't know why I noticed them, but his nails were perfectly oval, his cuticles impeccably tended to, and not a speck of dry skin anywhere along the palms that cupped the glass of whatever he was drinking.

I didn't make it a point to chit chat with random men. It was Vegas after all. Everyone had an angle. Besides, he'd interrupted my mental wish list of what I could buy with my winnings. Every well-known designer had a store here. In my head I was living out my wildest *Sex in the City* fantasies with bags upon bags of designer things.

"I debated coming over here." He chuckled. "I noticed your shirt while you were playing. My vanity doesn't want to admit that I'm old enough to remember that movie."

He signaled the bartender, and ordered himself some kind of something with a date on it. More than likely, it probably impressed people who actually drank. I wasn't one of those people. *I* presently sipped from a "Screaming Orgasm" that the bartender passed to me with a cheeky grin. While I had zero idea what ingredients made up the drink, it tasted like bad decisions, and went down with the ease of a cherry cola.

"Well, to quote the film," I giggled, pulling the straw into my mouth, *"how very."*

"Have you played long?" He nodded toward the gaming area.

"That's the first time I've ever had the balls to sit down at an actual table and play. I'm not much of a gambler and hate that you can blow a hundred dollars in a slot machine in three seconds flat."

"So, you prefer to slowly bleed out," he laughed.

He had a nice face. Weird observance I know. His chiseled

without being gaunt face could have been on a bust in the Louvre. He was that gorgeous. High cheekbones, pouty lips a woman would kill for, and such expressive eyes in the most unusual shade of ocean blue. It was as if he had been born straight out of the Adriatic Sea. Not that I'd ever seen it. The farthest I'd ever traveled was the Dominican Republic for a bachelorette party. One day I'd make it to Europe and see all the things.

"More like I want to enjoy having someone crawl into my pants and take all my money."

The hand holding his expensive libation stopped halfway up to his mouth. He turned toward me and smirked. The look in his eyes—shit, I felt tingly everywhere. Then I realized how laden with innuendo my comment had been.

"Not like that." I laughed, trying to cover my embarrassment. "I want to play for a while before bottoming out."

He shook his head and sipped from his glass. Jesus. I did it again.

"Playing by myself got boring. I saw a bunch of guys at that table, and the risk seemed minimal, so I figured why not see how I would fare with a group of five? I think I did pretty well for my first go. I emptied most of them. You saw my pot. It's more than I could have ever expected."

For long moments the only sounds were the incessant dinging of the slot machines, the cacophony of shouts of both glee and disbelief, and the thumping bass coming from the speakers. I replayed what I'd just said in my head and internally groaned. Somehow, everything I said to this stranger sounded dirty.

"I'm Harlow."

I turned and offered my hand. As soon as I did it, I wondered if I should have. But it seemed strange to exchange at least fifteen minutes worth of conversation and not know his name.

Those hands I'd been admiring earlier were unbelievably soft. He cradled my palm in his, smiling as our skin touched. My booze-addled brain sent all kinds of fluttery feelings through my system. Like a simple polite smile and handshake was equivalent to sonnets written in my honor.

"*Greetings and Salutations,* Harlow. I'm Cash."

"Cash?" I asked.

Obviously, I'd focused far too long on the fact he'd volleyed back a *Heathers* line to me. Which, in Harlow-land, was essentially a marriage proposal. Working movie quotes into everyday conversation was my love language.

"That's your real name?"

I watched him set his glass back down on the bar, reach behind him and pull out his wallet. Just my luck. I found someone who can engage in a verbal volley with me, and my obvious inability to flirt, already pushed him off.

"I'm sorry, it's just such an usual name."

I tried to backpedal, seeing him pull a credit card. Instead of throwing it on the bar in annoyance as I expected him to, he handed it to me. I must have looked totally confused to him. He pointed toward the name listed on the bottom of his AMEX.

"Cash Cole Murray," he said.

I looked between the name on the card and those ocean eyes of his. Once again, his eyes showed only mirth, and that mouth of his tilted up in a smirk. The room suddenly felt warmer as if someone painted my entire body—especially my face and neck— in the heat of the summer sun.

"According to my parents, I was more than likely conceived at a Johnny Cash concert."

I'd been about to make some comment about that little piece of knowledge when a blonder, younger version of Cash, interrupted our conversation.

"There you are. One minute you were standing next to me and the next you disappeared. C'mon, Beck wants to go eat."

The guy at Cash's shoulder had to be a brother. They had nearly identical faces with the exception being the non-Cash version was sandy-blonde and very tan. He looked like he could be the Coppertone baby all grown up.

"My youngest brother," Cash gestured with his glass toward him, "Harris."

Harris nodded in my direction with a noncommittal 'hey.' Cash cleared his drink, then threw a hundred on the table, making eye contact with the bartender and signaling he intended to cover both of our drinks.

"I hope to see you around, Harlow."

I barely got out a 'thanks for the drink!' before he and his brother disappeared into the melee on the casino floor.

CHAPTER 3

CASH 

loved my brothers. Vacations with the four of us? Rarely happens. I couldn't even remember the last time we'd all been home together for the holidays. Usually, at least one of us was absent. In years past, it was Beckett, Presley, or Harris, depending on where they were in their educational or professional careers and what swimming tournament they competed in. But I wasn't an innocent victim. More holidays than I cared to count I also called my parents with an excuse why I wouldn't be home.

As much as I wanted to soak in every minute of every hour with my brothers, I couldn't get the innocent little Harlow out of my head. God, had she been charming! I barely heard the conversation going around me. I preferred to get lost in easily the eleventh replay of our little tête-à-tête at the bar. Her innocent innuendos, one after the other. How each ratcheted up how flustered she became.

"What do you mean, you're going back to your room?" Harris was practically apoplectic. "It's not even ten o'clock!"

Beckett pushed off the table and shrugged. Not that anyone needed an explanation from him, but I knew he wasn't actually planning on going to sleep once he got back there. More than likely, he wanted some semblance of privacy for a bit with Lane. He had it bad.

"You really need to ask her to marry you already, my brother." I clapped him on his back as we walked toward the front of the casino. "The two of you are so hot for each other I get a sunburn every time I'm around you."

Beckett looked over his shoulder to gauge how far away our brothers were. With a sheepish grin, he pulled out a cream-colored box with the word *Graff* written in elegant script across the top. Shit. He'd leapt past all the standards: Tiffany, Harry Winston, Cartier and went straight for royalty.

"I didn't want her to accidentally find it," he explained. "But I also didn't want to leave it in the hotel. I've had it for weeks trying to think of the perfect way to ask."

My brother was a cocky motherfucker. You don't get to become one of the best swimmers in the world and not develop a very healthy infatuation with one's own abilities. Of course, that had been his downfall as well. A public intoxication at the Olympic Games that had him taking a piss in the Olympic Fountain all caught on camera. For a while after the scandal, though, he seemed to relish in being swimming's bad boy. Until he met Lane. Dating her had softened him somehow. He no longer walked around like the world owed him something.

"I definitely wouldn't ask her while you're Facetiming her, cock in hand, getting ready to jerk off to her strutting around in lingerie for you."

"You're such an asshole." The back of his hand landed against my chest with enough force to make me grunt. "Obviously, I'm not proposing now. Just in the very near future. And when I do, I'll need you to come to San Diego and stand up at my wedding."

There weren't any words. I had plenty of them in my arsenal. But a touching moment like that sandwiched into a blink-and-you-miss-it span of time as everyone went their separate ways for the evening? I couldn't say all the things I wanted to in the allotted gasp of time. Instead, I just hugged him before he hopped in an Uber and headed back to our hotel.

Harris and Presley had been right behind us. I said goodbye to Beckett, turned, and they were gone. Swallowed by the crowd. I didn't even have a text from them. I guess they assumed that if Beckett was going to bed, so was the oldest Murray brother. Fuck that.

Caesars always had great action on holiday weekends. I made my way over there figuring at the very least I could hang out in the sports book. I'd sent Presley and Harris a message in our brother's group chat, but had yet to hear from them. Not that I expected to. With as many people as there were in the casinos, it would be a miracle if they even had a signal.

As if the fates themselves shone a bright beam of golden light in front of me, I spotted Harlow standing in front of the Louis Vuitton shop along the underground walkway. I barely recognized her from behind. Harlow traded the messy bun and jeans from earlier to an elegant ensemble and styled hair that cascaded down her back. Where earlier her hair had looked nondescript brown, beneath the lights there were the prettiest hints of caramel. As if the sun had kissed her the moment she was born, imbuing the soft colors of morning light onto the crown of her head. Standing as she was, beneath the high wattage bulbs intended to entice shoppers to windows, she couldn't have been more beautiful. And that hair. The things I wanted to do with it. I could easily wrap its length around my hand three-fold.

"They close in about ten minutes." I told her.

I sauntered up next to where she stood, casually tucking my hands in my pockets. I had zero faith I could keep my hands to myself. I needed to know if those luscious curls felt as soft as they looked.

"If you're planning on buying something, best pull that trigger."

"I can't decide." She sighed, sounding like a governor in the midst of deciding whether or not to stay an execution.

"While I understand the desire to own a status symbol, personally, I'd keep walking. Louis Vuitton in my opinion has become watered down in its esteem and value. Too many people carry around really convincing fakes. So much so that those who *care* about *those things* spend their energies minimizing everyone else as if they're the only ones who could possibly own the real thing."

I felt her gaze on my profile. Gaze, of course, was a nice way of saying I felt the molten focus of Medusa boiling my skin as we stood. I tended to do that. Give unsolicited advice. It wasn't intentional. Sometimes I got too comfortable with strangers.

It lingered. The heat of her stare. She was waiting for me to look at her. It was my funeral if I did. Fuck it.

"Let me guess, we would better spend the money feeding the homeless, or perhaps donating to a women's shelter?"

God, she was cute when her hackles came up. It was her nose. That perfectly proportioned nose crinkled with offense. A perfect accessory to the mouth winding up to give me a dress down. Lest we forget those eyes—an enticing brown-green that reminded me of moss—squinted in judgment. I almost wanted to continue to bait her so I could see how riled up she'd get. But this was Vegas and time moved both fast and slow here. I needed to make the most of every second I had.

"I mean, if that's your jam, sure." I shrugged, turning back to survey the window display. "I just think if you're going to blow a wad of money on something, it should be more personal. Something that will make *you* feel good."

She shifted, so she was directly in my line of sight. My cock stiffened at the asset hugging lace top she swapped her t-shirt for. I imagined wrapping my hands around her waist, pulling her against me, and kissing that indignant little scowl right off her lips.

"How do you know a Louis Vuitton bag wouldn't *make me feel good*?"

I could think of a million ways to make her feel good and

none of them had anything to do with buying an overpriced junk holder.

"Because you'd have marched in there, plunked down your credit card and confidently pointed to the one you wanted. Instead, you're standing out here, allowing time to decide for you."

I pointed to the door that beeped as it slid closed. Time was up for Cinderella. No more magic. She didn't even look upset. They'd reopen again at nine the next morning as their sign cheerfully reminded everyone.

"It's a lot of money. I'm weighing the pros and the cons."

Her eyebrow raised in challenge, though the smirk threatening to spread into a smile contradicted the sass of that well shaped little peak.

"This is true. And found money which is the best kind. You know that's why they have these shops right where the action is. Because it's a win-win-win for everyone. The casinos loosen their holds every once in a while, and let people walk away with big wins. They know that means fewer taxes they have to pay at the end of the year. Incidentally, they also are keenly aware that nearly ninety-seven percent of gambling winners won't make it out of Las Vegas without re-gambling it, or spending their winnings on some kind of shoot the moon purchase they normally wouldn't buy in their day-to-day lives. That found money then, of course, gets plunked down with little thought into a shop within the casino, where said casino gets a chunk of the overhead. I mean, sure, they lost it in the casino, but they make it back in rent from the store.

"All of it, the rent, the casinos, the hotels, the restaurants, the cabs, everything that keeps Vegas running, continued to feed right back into the nearly trillion-dollar machine. So really, the thousand dollars they lost on your big win probably actually nets them a decent chunk of change."

My words hung in the air like little speech bubbles. I felt her eyes assess my face, taking a slow journey from my mouth to my eyes and back again. I'd like to believe it was that cool assessment that had my mouth continuing to flow like Mount Vesuvius.

"Which brings me back to the original discussion. If your purchase is only going to end up *helping* the casino make *more* money, shouldn't you buy something with that windfall that will make you smile every time you see it?"

"What are you? The Convention and Tourism bureau?" She huffed a laugh. "I think you may want to seek alternative employment. Vegas seems to have jaded you."

Like that arrow didn't strike true. I hated Vegas as much as I hated Atlantic City. I only came because my brothers asked me to.

I shrugged feeling sheepish.

"I just meant that if you're going to buy something here, in Vegas, and not bring your winnings home with you, why not get something that you really love."

She looked at me for long moments. The way her eyes bore into mine it felt strangely intimate. As if she had unearthed all of my long-buried feelings and insecurities and quietly examined each one and stored them in her mind for later evaluation.

"What would you get?" she asked.

It felt like a whisper. A quiet entreaty to help her decide. I didn't know if it really was so, or I just imagined it to be. Regardless, I pointed to a shop four doors down. La Perla. My favorite. My brother wasn't the only one with a thing for lingerie. In fact, the reason he had a thing for lingerie is probably because *I* was the one who had all the lingerie magazines in our shared bedroom growing up.

"Well, Mr. Las Vegas, here is a thing you clearly don't know about your beloved city. Stores like that one," she tossed her chin in the direction of the La Perla, "prefer to keep my kind out of it. In fact, I don't think there is a single store in Las Vegas—other than say maybe in the mall—that sells any form of intimates to people like me."

People like her? I had no idea what she insinuated. But I unintentionally struck a chord. Though there was a fire burning in those moss-colored eyes, I saw just behind that, barely discernible beneath the ire, was a softer emotion that I couldn't figure out. There was a curly ringlet of hair that teased along her brow line. It softly rocked back and forth as she spoke, as if it were a boat tossed around in a storm.

"Ironic given they bill Las Vegas as the City of Sin for everyone to imbibe in."

Her eyes widened the closer my hand got to her face. I gathered that tiny tendril between my fingers and repositioned it behind her ear. The breath she exhaled sounded like a sigh but was a dichotomy to the ire behind her words.

"Unless you aren't a size six. Then it's the accessory walls for you."

She waved her hand toward Louis Vuitton once again, and it clicked. Rather, it slammed into me like a two by four. The only things she could buy in Vegas if she wanted to "splurge" would be accessories.

It was that look. The indiscernible one. It called to me like a mermaid called to a sailor. I recognized that song. The one that said you were less than because of other people's opinions. It pulled me into her orbit, damn the consequences. I heard the smallest gasp when I stepped into her space. Felt the soft shake of her exhaled breath.

"Vegas doesn't know what it's missing, then."

Not my smoothest line, but I admit I was rusty. And I honestly didn't know what to say that would cauterize that wound. That's what it was. A wound. Something that told me she'd been used to being cast aside.

"You're incredibly sexy."

She smelled as if she'd been baking in a cupcake shop. The ringlets of her hair teased my senses with something soothing, and warm, and sweet. As if expecting her to bolt like a frightened rabbit, my hand hovered just below the clasp of her bra. I wanted to pull her against me, to feel her lush curves, but didn't want to risk ruining the crystalline purity of the moment.

"Anyone who has ever said otherwise, is a moron."

Her eyebrow arched in tandem with the slightest quirk of her lips. "I guess that says a lot about society then, doesn't it?"

It was too much. The intoxicating combination of innocence and sass, bottled together with a luscious body that made me want to lose myself in her softness. In that moment, nothing else mattered more than learning more about the alluring creature standing in front of me.

Between my fingers her hair felt like the softest blanket, the silkiest set of sheets, the coolest breeze against my skin. Have I ever touched anything like it? The moment our lips touched, she melted. The suppleness of her body pressed against my own, melding into all the places that zipped to life on a wave of adrenaline.

I'd expected her softness when I kissed her. Based on our interaction, I thought she'd be apprehensive. It lasted all of a millisecond before her mouth bit at my own, desperate to deepen whatever sensations she felt. Who was I to deny her that pleasure?

I held the back of her head in place and doubled down. Her fingernails traced enticing patterns in my hairline as she pressed herself against me. The little groan of surprise when I fed her my tongue stiffened my cock.

"Woah."

Her voice was barely a whisper. Those unicorn covered fingernails traced the lips I'd just been worshipping. Her phone began to chirp from her back pocket just as I readied myself to dive in for round two.

"Sorry." She bit her lip, the dewy flush that dotted her cheeks moments before blooming into a full blush. "It's my sister."

Surprised she had a signal, I passively checked my phone while she told her sister she was at the shops inside Caesars.

> Harris: wtf did you go?

> Harris: idk where you ran off to but we're going to the Cosmopolitan.

> Harris: Maybe I can find some hot piece that wants a one-night stand with me too 😉

He was such a tool. Beckett and Lane met in Vegas at the Cosmopolitan, hooked up, and assumed they would never see one another again. Then Beckett went off and bought a company and surprise! Guess who worked for said company but little Laney Deveraux—soon to be Murray whenever Beckett got up the nerve to ask.

It was nice to see him so damn happy. Jesus, he'd become too beholden to USA Swimming for so many years, he'd practically lost himself to the sport. Like those words didn't strike true with me. Losing myself. Forgetting who I was. What my purpose was. I'd been rudderless for years. A stone that gathered no moss. And what did I have to show for those things? I was three years away from forty and living like a twenty-one-year-old bachelor.

Hell, even Harris, for all his youthful exuberance, possessed a clearer path than I did. Of all the Murray brothers, I was probably the least successful, and had little to show for the last fifteen years of my life. Sure, I had friends on the Poker circuit. If I mentioned my name to the right people, I'd probably get a comped meal or at least some enthusiastic hand shaking. But gamblers weren't exactly the most reliable friends to have. And pull away the glitz and glamor of a vacation destination like Las Vegas, and look at its underbelly—of the day-to-day lives of people who lived and breathed their next game—it definitely wasn't a Disney song, that's for sure.

"I'm so sorry. I have to go." Harlow bit her lip and held up her phone. "My sister is having a crisis and I need to get back to the hotel."

I could feel a ceaseless string of text messages from Harris vibrating in my pocket. The kid seriously needed to learn how to make his thoughts concise and send a single text message. The one sentence one offs drove me batty.

"We're staying at the same hotel. Let me at least split a cab with you." I offered, as she powered through the casino toward the front doors of the hotel.

"No, it's okay. I'm going to walk. It's not that far."

A battle raged inside me. Other than a single kiss and some friendly banter the day before, I knew nothing about her. She wasn't beholden to me. But whatever conversation she'd had with her sister creased her face with worry.

"Look, Harlow," I looped my arm through hers, trying to slow her down enough to have a sensible conversation before she shot off blindly into the melee. "You look upset. I'm no one, of course. But I would feel much better knowing you got to the hotel safely and quickly. Consider it a favor to me."

Her lip was getting abused between her teeth as she tried to decide. Thankfully, we kept walking toward the valet circle while she did. And, right in front of where we stood, a cab sat idling.

"It's like they knew we had to get somewhere quickly." I pointed toward the attendant holding open the door with a smile.

CHAPTER 4

Harlow

"That tiny little dweeb! Of all the things I need to worry about right now, this! This? Unbelievable!"

My sister, Lennox, hadn't stopped shouting, stomping around our hotel room, and railing against her asshole neighbor for twenty minutes. When she called me, she was in hysterics. I could barely make out what the problem was. Initially.

Eventually, she said she'd been served a demand letter by the HOA to the tune of seven thousand dollars. When Lennox woke up from her alcohol nap, her phone was filled with urgent voicemails from our mom. I guess the fine resulted from violating some arbitrary rule about landscaping. Now she'd progressed past crying to angry rants, continually repeating the same thing over again.

Unfortunately, I had a hard time focusing on her crisis. Cash and that kiss were on an infinite loop in my head. I certainly wasn't a virgin, but Jesus, no one ever kissed me like that. He kissed as if he was sin itself. He was lips, teeth, and tongue. The sensations he elicited I never knew were possible from kissing alone.

Even now, nearly thirty minutes later, my lips still tingled. They weren't the only thing that tingled. He'd taken a pair of paddles to my libido, shouted 'Clear!,' and awakened feelings that had been long dead and decomposing.

Every so often I'd catch the subtle tease of his cologne on my skin, and that would rewind the tawdry remembrances of that kiss and set me off on a firestorm of need all over again. While Lennox continued to rail about the "little Napoleon" who lived next door to her.

"If his biggest concern in the entire world is me using prairie grass in my front yard, the guy clearly needs to get laid. What a loser. Honestly, Harlow. Who the fuck gives two shits about how my lawn is tended? Isn't that my business?"

Speaking of lawns… I wondered off hand if Cash preferred a bare landscape, a nice tight trim, or if he preferred exploring in a jungle in its natural habitat. That kiss affirmed my belief that he would rock my damn world. Assuming, of course, that we would ever find ourselves in a situation where he spread me across a bed, or… shit… across a poker table! *That* would be hot as hell.

Focus Harlow.

"We'll figure it out, Lennox. I promise I'll do anything I can to help."

"Help?"

Lennox's voice went up a full octave. She was unraveling. Her eyes bugged, that vein between her eyes on her forehead pulsed.

"Do you have seven thousand dollars somewhere I don't know about?"

She knew I didn't. I barely made enough to cover my rent and car payment. Working for the opera was cool and all, but Stage Managers made shit.

"Where the hell am I supposed to get seven thousand dollars? Teddy and I barely get by with the pittance Danny is required to pay us."

Cash: How's the sibling emergency?

. . .

I had to tell my face that smiling in the middle of Lennox's crisis would not be supportive. But when he asked me for my phone number on the cab ride over to the hotel, I thought he was just being polite. Like since he kissed me, the least he could do was give me some hope that *maybe* we'd reconnect over the next few days.

> Me: 🦇 She's still pretty upset.

> Cash: I won't disturb. Just wanted to make sure you made it up to your hotel room okay

> Cash: Those $5 poker tables are hard to pass up I hear 😊

Seeing his name on my phone skittered an army of little ants dancing through my bloodstream. Was it possible to come simply from delight? Because getting that message shot bliss through me so quickly, it felt like an orgasm of the mind.

"Everyone said, '*Move to Naperville!* Good schools, kid friendly, great neighborhoods.' Sure. Great neighborhoods. Until you decide to buy a cute little ranch on a quiet cul-de-sac next to a tiny little man with an oversized truck, and an even bigger ego. Said man somehow knows the HOA laws backward and forward. Fucking prairie grass. Who the hell cares what I planted? At least I have plants!"

Every time I thought she'd wind down, she found a second wind and started railing all over again. I wish I had an answer for her. Truly. It wasn't fair. This vacation was supposed to be a way for her to relax.

"We'll figure it out." I told her. "I will help however I can."

Eventually, Lennox ran out of steam and fell asleep. Rather than sit in a silent hotel room, I made my way back to the casino floor. My body still buzzed. My sleeping beauty lady parts wanted more now that Cash woke them up from a years-long coma.

Quite honestly, even with my last relationship, they got more solo attention than from my ex. He pumped like a rabbit, and he certainly never kissed like Cash. I glanced at my watch. Nearly midnight and still my lips pulsed with the ghost of it.

As if testing the fates, I approached a poker table and placed a fifty on the pile. I glanced around the room as if that one act would be enough to *Beetlejuice* Cash back into existence. There wasn't a sign of him anywhere. I checked my phone, just in case for some odd reason he'd decided to text me at that very moment. Nothing.

"You're on the button, lady."

The man seated across from me impatiently huffed as I collected my cards and put my five-dollar chip into the pot. It was past midnight, yet the casino was a sensory overload of sound and light. I couldn't look anywhere without getting distracted and found hyper focusing on the game I played was soothing.

I'd come downstairs for many reasons. I hadn't been tired and didn't want to disturb Lennox, who clearly needed sleep. Of course, coming here I'd hoped to run into Cash without being so obvious about wanting to see him again. Getting pulled into another round of Hold 'Em, though, hadn't really been part of the plan.

"I'm out."

One of the last three men at the table threw his cards down. His shirt was dingy, like he'd purchased it at a resale shop and didn't bother to wash it before putting it on. He wore oversized seventies style glasses and was missing one of his eye teeth, which made him look almost horse like.

"What are you, some kind of shark?"

While the words sounded like a joke, his eyes missed that memo. Stunned to see such annoyance from a stranger, I looked down at my winnings. Shock. That was a great word to sum up my feelings. In the evening's progression, I'd won nearly four hundred dollars.

"How often do you play?"

The man seated directly to my right asked, readjusting the sunglasses under his baseball cap.

"To be honest, this is only my second time at an actual table."

Both he and the dealer looked at me in shock.

"This is total beginner's luck." I chuckled, rounding up my chips and preparing to clear the table. "When I'm in a casino, which is honestly close to never, I play video poker. Sometimes at Christmas I'll play with my uncles down in the basement while we wait for presents. But that's the extent of my poker playing."

I placed a twenty-dollar chip on the table for the dealer, signaling I was out as well.

"You should join the tournament." The dealer suggested, pointing toward a poster over his shoulder. "Buy in is two hundred and fifty dollars. Split pot for the last table, up to ten grand."

Ten thousand dollars? It had to be a sign. Why else would I suddenly have the urge to sit down at a poker table that randomly advertised a tournament right after promising Lennox I would help her figure out how to take care of her HOA fines.

"You'll need to sign up by ten a.m. Tournament starts at four o'clock tomorrow afternoon for the first elimination rounds. Championship rounds are on Sunday."

Three hundred and sixty-seven dollars is what I came away with at the poker table. Found money. It didn't even belong to me in the sense that I hadn't worked for it or earned it. If I played in the tournament and lost, I wouldn't have lost anything more than what I'd just won. I even still had the Louis Vuitton purse money, less the fifty dollars I'd used to play.

"Can you direct me to where I sign up?"

Good idea or bad, at least I could say I tried something that was within my power to help Lennox out of a crisis.

CHAPTER 5

CASH 

While usually if asked I will vociferously proclaim I can still hang with the twenty somethings. Thanks to Harris, I discovered this is in fact a lie. Harris has more staying power than an energizer bunny. I finally waved the white flag at three in the morning, right around the time Harris and Presley got their second wind.

I was also the only one, apparently, that appreciated a good sleep in after a night of drinking. None of my brothers required the same. The texts started pouring in just after seven o'clock.

Harris: We're hungry.

Harris. U up?

Harris: Bfast?

Harris: Seriously.

Harris: Pres & I need food now 🌍

Me: Jesus. How are the two of you awake already?

Harris: We're gonna hit the buffet in 15

Harris: Pres says he wants to shower 1st

Me: You know it's entirely possible to send all of this in one text message. No need to hit "send" after every thought. FYI.

Group Text from Beckett: Hey guys. So I flew back to San Diego last night. I had a question I wanted to ask Lane and I couldn't wait. I'll be back in the A.M. Promise.

Harris: You FLEW BACK? Like, on Southwest?

Since we all lived in different states, we obviously had converged in Las Vegas as the meet point. I couldn't even picture Mr. Olympian on a Southwest flight. I thought he and Harris drove to Vegas.

Group Text from Beckett: um, not quite. I asked ESPN if I could borrow their plane. They were in Vegas for the fights.

Presley: Must be nice to be such a celebrity that ESPN hands over their billion-dollar jet to borrow.

Beckett: I may have promised them they'd have an exclusive with us, tomorrow.

Presley: 😌

Harris: 😨

Me: 🧑

Beckett: Great talking with the three of you. Such a deep and meaningful convo. I'll be back by 8a. Presley our interview is at 10.

"He didn't even *ask* if I *wanted* to do an interview."

The amount of food that both he and Harris piled on their plates. You would think they hadn't eaten hundred-dollar steaks for dinner last night, and also ordered nachos, wings, and garlic fries at the diner to "soak up" the alcohol.

"You seemed pretty interested in it yesterday when he mentioned they were texting him with the request."

"Yeah, but that was before Pres faced the reality of actually having to not look like an asshole on TV and fucking up his new job before he even gets a nameplate affixed to the door." Harris laughed, shoving a syrup covered piece of bacon in his mouth.

Just watching the pair of them eat made me nauseous. I could barely handle the toast and fruit I'd grabbed. With four of us, it always fascinated me how similar Presley and Harris were, and how totally different the pair were to Beckett and me. Presley and Harris were both charming, the life of the party, happy-go-lucky, roll with the punches type of people.

Where Beckett and I both had a fair share of people call us "intense," for different reasons. He was driven. Saw a goal and crushed it every time. It was rare he failed, because any stumble he faced, he took as an opportunity to better himself. He played the long game. That's why he'd been such an outstanding athlete, and now a commentator.

My focus and intensity were similar but different. I needed immediate gratification. I hated playing the long game in anything. If I couldn't have it right now, it wasn't worth having.

Between that and more than likely some undiagnosed neurodivergence, it made me incredibly awkward growing up. I was the video game kid who played for long hours until I figured out how to best it. The one who spent hours readying a board game for some super complex game that only my brothers would have the patience and tolerance to play with me. Adults loved me at parties. They'd laugh and tell my mom what a precocious child I was because I could sit and have these long, esoteric conversations with them about the stock market, behavioral economics, and rational expectations.

While Dad's business friends loved I could discuss recession proof portfolios, thirteen-year-old kids at school dances were not so impressed. However, being a wallflower allowed me the power of observation. I learned everyone had a tell in every situation. Enter the world of poker. When you combined intense focus, and the power of observation in a nerdy kid that didn't have many friends, poker was the perfect haven.

"I can't imagine why Beckett wants to lose you as a roommate," Presley volleyed back.

While it earned an ill-disguised snicker from me, poor Harris looked genuinely hurt.

"What do you mean *lose me as a roommate?* He has no complaints in the roommate department. In fact, when his life was in the shitter, I was the only one who went running with the paper towel and the Windex to help him figure out how to clean it back up."

"Alright," I stopped the bickering before it turned into an avalanche. "The two of you are giving me flashbacks to bunk beds at Mom and Dad's house. That is the last fucking thing I want to think about with a hangover. My god, you're twenty-three and twenty-seven, respectively. Act your age."

The pair turned at nearly the same time, identical smiles appearing on their faces.

"You know the best cure for that?" Harris suggested, pulling the drink menu from between the salt, pepper, and sugar on the table.

"Hair of the Dog!" Presley finished, clapping Harris on the shoulder, signaling for the waitress.

When did I become so old?

CHAPTER 6

Harlow

n the magic haze of the middle of the night, being my sister's gallant knight seemed like the best idea in the world. Now? In the bright, glaring light of morning, seeing my name listed on the poker tournament player's board didn't seem all that brilliant anymore. I was assigned to table 13 according to the chart. I didn't think Vegas *did* the number 13. Maybe the unluckiest number would be my lucky charm.

Technically, I *could* still back out for one more hour and seven minutes. Lennox didn't even know yet. We'd really not said much since waking up. She talked to her son, Teddy, and my mom as soon as she was coherent. It took her forever to figure out what she wanted to do for breakfast.

"God, how is it so hot and it's not even eight in the morning?"

Lennox woke up with the most sparkling personality that carried through our morning breakfast out by the pool. She pulled at the tank top she wore as if she could lose any more clothing. After Teddy was born, before their marriage started careening toward divorce, he'd bought her a boob job for Christmas. Most of the time, she never even bothered with a bra because they stood up all on their own without the need of wires and spandex. Me, on the other hand, with double d's, needed a wing and a prayer to make them look anywhere as gorgeous as hers were. She'd have no problem finding something sexy in La Perla, Agent Provocateur, or Fleur du Mal. Not like I'd spent hours scouring their websites before I went to bed to see if any of them had inclusive sizing. Spoiler alert, they didn't. Why did a man who I'd only met yesterday get so much space in my brain?

"Do you know that guy?"

My sister pointed with the straw of her iced matcha tea toward a group of men making their way toward the pool. No. Those words did not quite explain the attention they commanded. Three men in varying states of leanly chiseled, sauntered across the pool deck, undressing as they walked, tossed their t-shirts and towels on a few lounge chairs while kicking their sandals off beneath them. Cash and his brothers were drool worthy. I couldn't stop gawking. Even forgot that Lennox asked me a question.

"Earth to Lo." She waved her hand in front of my face. "I take it, you know them then?"

I shook my head.

"Just the one in the green shorts."

"Mr. Sunglasses. Yes, he was the one who waved as he walked by."

"His name is Cash. I met him at the hotel bar yesterday. The other two are his brothers. I met the tall drink of water for a split-second before they left for dinner, but I forget his name."

"Cash as in money?"

"Cash as in Johnny Cash. Cash Cole Murray." I smiled, remembering him pulling his AMEX out to show me, "his parents apparently conceived him either *at* a Johnny Cash concert or after it? The details are fuzzy. But there was a concert, and a conception, and then nine months later, a little Cash Cole."

"Cash Cole definitely is not little... anywhere."

"No," I agreed, taking a sip from my own iced coffee. "None of them appear to be little anywhere."

. . .

Cash: You joining us in the pool or are you just going to ogle me from afar? 😉

"Wait. Full stop. He has your cell phone number?"

Lennox practically screeched when Cash's name popped across the top of my cell phone. I hadn't been able to grab it fast enough. The woman was an eagle eye.

"I told you, we met at the bar. We exchanged numbers in case our paths crossed again."

I tried to play it off like it was no big deal. Why would it be a big deal that I randomly had a phone number of some guy presently popping out of the water and swiping his hair off his face like a damn body wash commercial? It was completely normal for people to exchange phone numbers. Well, other people. Let's be honest. He was probably the first number anyone had given me in a very long time.

Me: Aw, so sad. I'm not wearing my bathing suit. Guess I'll have to take a raincheck.

"What does he want?" Lennox asked.

"For us to come swimming." I laughed.

"There is no way I am parading out in a bathing suit with these mom thighs and jiggly skin in front of those three specimens of perfection. The last thing I need is them wondering when the pool became an ocean."

Lennox was a size ten. She'd never in her entire life been overweight, even slightly. What her comment really meant was that *I,* in my size twenty clothes, should feel embarrassed in front of them.

I'd just fortified the steel in my spine to point out this fact, when the scrolling televisions announcing various promotions in the casino caught her attention.

"Harlow, why did I just see your name flash on the screen?"

I turned in the direction to where she pointed, missing what it said.

"Oh! Did I win something? Like a raffle?"

"Not quite," she said, while the slides cycled through. "It said something about a poker tournament."

"Oh! From winning yesterday? I didn't think a nine hundred-and eighty-eight-dollar pot, coupled with three hundred something would be enough to make their little announcement screen."

The words died a quiet death as I saw the slide she referenced. The one that said there were less than thirty minutes left to secure a table in the *Pays to be a Patriot Hold 'Em Tournament.* There was my name. Listed on table 13. It had filled a bit more. There was only one seat left at my table, and tables fourteen, fifteen and sixteen, showed on the screen with nearly full tables as well.

"So, funny story. When you passed out yesterday, I got bored with video poker and sat down at a real live table. I won almost a thousand dollars! Then all the stuff happened with the HOA and my exciting news just kind of didn't seem so important at that moment. Then after you went to bed, I couldn't sleep. So I hung out at the poker table to kill some time till I got tired. I planned on just playing a round or two. And wouldn't you know it? Another three hundred dollars and some change! The dealer suggested I enter that tournament. Get this. The pot if I make it to the final table? It will pay off your whole HOA bill. The whole thing! Just from playing poker!"

Rather than say anything, Lennox gathered her mane of caramel colored hair into a ponytail, twisting it around her fingers and tucking it into itself to form a bun.

"I figured that even if I lost, it wasn't my money to begin with. It's the casinos. So, all I'm doing is, you know, doing what they hope I do with it. Spend it. At their casino. Where it just makes them more money."

I shrugged as if that would be the end of the conversation. I knew Lennox better than that though. Her brand of silence marked the passage of every fight from childhood to adulthood. She gold medaled in silent treatment longevity. Eventually, she'd give me a dress down. Once she gathered her thoughts.

"I can't take your money."

Of all the things I expected from Lennox, soft and conciliatory wasn't it.

"My problems aren't yours to solve. And I don't want you putting yourself in harm's way over my debts."

"Harm? Where's the harm? It's not even my money. I bought-in with the *casino's* own money."

She sighed. I hated when she did it. It said so many words without needing to. That she thought I'd made a mistake. That I was just the silly little sister needing saving again. I was missing her point and spending money I should use on myself. Too many things were in that damn sigh.

"Look," I reached across our little café table and took her hand in mine. "You're my ride or die. It's been that way since we were kids. If I needed seven thousand dollars and you had the means to give it to me, I know you would without question."

"Oh Lo... I don't know about this. How much money are you going to lose?"

"Doesn't matter. The money's already spent and nonrefundable. And apparently all those games for quarters playing against Uncle Mac and Uncle Tim paid off because I did surprisingly well last night!"

I looked up and saw him and his brothers lounging on deck chairs, glistening like swimming's version of the Cullens in the sunshine. He wanted to see me naked. Cash Cole Murray wanted me to jump in that pool naked as the day I was born. And part of me wanted to. Not with a million people milling about, and certainly not in the age of camera phones and social media. But the thought of skinny dipping with *just* Cash? Yes, please.

CHAPTER 7

CASH 

Harlow and her sister were still in whatever tiff they'd been the night before. I looked over a few times and saw Harlow's sister gesticulating wildly toward the casino. Even my flirtatious text about going skinny dipping with her hadn't pressed pause on whatever they argued about.

"You've had your nose buried in your phone all morning." Presley playfully slapped my chest, pulling me back into the conversation. "What gives? You are the first to eschew such plebeian forms of communication as the lowly text message."

"Only with the two of you." I volleyed. "There is nothing worse than having a stilted conversation with two people obsessed with the "send message" button. How hard is it to just type out a whole response in one go and hit send."

"So you can read our response while we continue to type. It's a courtesy, really." Harris chimed in.

"Don't try to deflect from the original question," Presley pressed. "Who are you talking to? I doubt it's Beckett. His text this morning seemed to suggest he would be incommunicado for the day. Mom and Dad don't text, and neither of us have a phone call from them, and you know they always make the rounds and talk to each of us on the same day. I don't think you have any friends that would even be awake at this hour. So—out with it. Who is she?"

"It's the chick from the bar. The one from yesterday. When I came to get you for dinner." Harris hooted like a baboon, hiding his gaping maw of a smile behind his closed fist.

"You *approached a woman* at a bar and got her phone number?"

Presley shoved at my shoulder with an equally obnoxious smile. Did they think I was a celibate monk? I'd approached women before. I wasn't still the awkward thirteen-year-old afraid to ask Molly Templeton to dance with me.

"You know I am a fully functioning adult. I'm not even a virgin anymore."

I mimicked that blonde kid from that *Home Alone* movie in mock shock.

"Meh, debatable." Presley teased, "Do three useless pumps before you accidentally slipped out of your oversized condom and blew all over her leg really count as a sexual experience?"

"I begged Mom for a sister. Begged. And every single time she brought home another dick."

"Well, after you nearly drown Beckett, she probably figured she best make some backups," Harris joked.

Though it wasn't a joke. Beckett had actually almost died when we were kids. That's how the brothers Murray ended up in swim lessons in the first place. We'd been playing on the beach in Fort Myers, near our grandparent's house. Beck and I had been trying to build the biggest sandcastle ever—by little boy standards —and I suggested we make a moat. I told Beckett to take our bucket to the water and fill it up.

The undertow had been really strong. When Beckett bent over to try to get some water to fill our bucket, he overestimated the softness of the sand and pitched face first into the ocean. The pull of the undertow apparently was stronger than the floaties he wore on his arms, and he was sucked so far out so quickly. It happened so fast. Everyone rushed in to get him, but his lungs had already filled with water, and it took the lifeguards what seemed like forever to get him breathing again before the ambulance came and took him and my mom away.

After that, my mom insisted that the two of us learn how to swim and become good at it. Then as Presley and Harris joined the family, the same rules applied to them. Of course, three out of the four of us became really good at it. I was still riddled with the guilt of almost killing my best friend, and Beckett was still terrified of the ocean.

"I'll catch up with you guys later." I pushed off my chair and slid into my sandals.

The genial atmosphere disappeared, and I needed to move and distract myself from being weighed down with guilt again. I heard Presley slap Harris' arm as I walked away, calling him an asshole. I wasn't mad at him. He was the baby of the family and heard everything through the filter of other family remembrances.

Nearly all of them made it past the trauma of the experience now that we were in our late twenties and early thirties respectively; and were grateful to have survived it. They'd all arrived at the point where it wasn't a tragedy to talk about it. I never had. I don't know if I ever would. It haunted me. Still. Seeing that flash of blue swimming trunks and Power Ranger floaties. Hearing him call my name before getting sucked under and being helpless to do anything more than scream and point.

Harlow: I need your help

My pulse jumped. Not the text I expected to see. Especially as I spiraled into a dark place of feeling *helpless*. That had to be the reason I jumped at the chance to come to her aid.

Me: What's up?

Harlow: I may have done a dumb thing. Meet
me at the coffee shop by the dollar slots.

I was seven long strides from the very place that she paced,
twisting a strand of her hair while studying her phone screen like
there was about to be a pop quiz.

"Somehow I doubt you could do anything dumb."

Her head jerked up from her phone. The moment she saw
me, the tension in her eyes melted. Melted. Like I wasn't just some
asshole she met at the casino bar last night.

"I joined a poker tournament."

Okay. Maybe she was capable of dumb things. We all had our
weak moments.

"My sister owes a lot of money to her HOA. Money she
doesn't have. Her neighbor," she rolled her eyes heavenward
letting out a long, labored breath. "This guy, I don't know, has it
in for her or something and reported her for having some kind of
fucked up landscaping. She's a single mom, just got a divorce—
that's why we're in Vegas. I'm supposed to be cheering her up—
and this is the only way I think I can help."

The words sped up the more she talked. It didn't all make
sense, but I got the gist. She decided to slice open her jugular and
jump into a tank of sharks, with the hopeful outcome of not
being eaten alive. Great plan.

"And you need my help?"

I didn't think I'd told her anything about what I did. Who I
was. Why I hated Las Vegas and all the shiny, noisy, abundance of
this town.

"Based on the conversation last night, you know before we…"

she shrugged, the cutest blush working its way up her neck to her cheeks, "I figured you would know enough to maybe give me some pointers?"

That kiss. That's all it had been. A single kiss. Yet I may as well have called her Dr. Frankenstein because she'd hooked me up to a lightning bolt and shocked to life something inside of me. Something foreign. But I wanted to poke at it. Prod it like a kid with a stick who discovered a slug on the pavement.

"...know we just met...kind of desperate...promised I would do whatever I could to help."

I'd missed a piece of conversation while lost in my own thoughts. I could give her more than pointers. With enough time I could teach her everything I knew. All that I'd learned over the years in the poker circuit. But I really shouldn't be anywhere near poker tournaments. I'd sworn them off. I threw a nuclear bomb to my bridge in Vegas before I left.

She crossed her arms across her chest, biting at her lip. Those moss-colored eyes of hers brimmed with hope that I wouldn't flat out reject her plea for help.

They were going to eat her alive. She wouldn't make it out of the first round. These tiny tournaments the casinos used to draw people in over holiday weekends were packed with frat boys with too much bravado and the Las Vegas stereotype. The desperate guys who were "just one win" away from breaking even.

She didn't have enough experience to make it through an entire tournament. Which was exactly why she needed my help. She realized her deficiency and had reached out to me for help. Because she trusted me enough based on one mother fucking kiss to help her. Damn.

Between the innocence of the expression, that lip trapped between her teeth that *I* wanted to bite, and the sweet plea behind her rounded eyes, how could anyone not fall victim to her charms? Her face could have been stolen from Thelxiepeia herself– the siren with the face of an angel who could persuade men to do any number of things.

That was it! The solution to how we'd get her through the tournament.

"How willing are you to part with some of your winnings?" I asked her.

"Excuse me? You want me to *pay* you for your help? Thanks, but I'll figure it out on my own."

Her button nose scrunched with such a snotty little scowl that I nearly laughed in her face.

"No." I chuckled. "We need to go shopping. I have an idea on how we'll get you through that tournament."

I reached out and brushed a nonexistent hair off her forehead. The moment our skin touched, I felt it again. That strange electricity that I'd felt last night at the Forum Shops. She made my blood vibrate, but it wasn't unpleasant. I wanted to experience it over and over. Thankfully, my plan meant I'd be around her all day long and could drink in that electricity like an elixir.

CHAPTER 8

Harlow

"No way."

Cash and I spent the morning at the mall across the street from the hotel. Much to my surprise, they did in fact have quite a few stores that served *people like me*. Even more surprising? Cash walked into them like he owned the place. Picking outfits off of racks and holding them up for my approval without so much blinking an eye when I grabbed my size and added it to the pile in the dressing room.

"I told you, it's my mission to make you look so fuckable and delicious that every man in that room is going to forget he has a pile of money in front of him."

He ran the back of his hand down my cheek and my whole body shivered. You know what else shivered? My scared inner self who'd been hiding behind a curtain ashamed to just exist for too many years. She'd peeked out a few times during our shopping excursions. I swear every time he overtly flirted with me, she crooked a thumb at him, confusion dancing across her imagined face asking if this dude was for real.

"You might want to reel in those expectations, Mr. Murray. Not everyone is you."

I grabbed the red and black laced bustier from his grip and

shoved it back into the drawer he'd pulled it from. He'd wanted me to wear it with a pair of pleather leggings and fuck me boots. No one needed to see me exposing that much skin.

The laughter died when I looked up from the rack into an arctic sea.

"Take it back, Harlow."

"What? The shirt? Sorry, Cash, but no way. I have final veto and I say absolutely not."

"Fuck the shirt."

He crowded into my space. Even though he'd only stepped less than a full shoe length to where I stood, I felt boxed in. Surrounded.

"Someone did a number on your self-confidence."

His warm hands wrapped around my waist. I winced. He was *touching* me on the area of my body that brought me the most shame and discomfort. As desperate as I was to pull away from his touch, the warmth of his tone settled me.

"A lot of someones," I admitted.

He pulled me against his chest and kissed my forehead. The gesture was pure comfort. Something unexpected from a near stranger, but it settled the sharp edges of my nerves.

"Don't let an industry designed to sow recrimination and shame in every woman from the moment they hit puberty, determine your self worth. *You* light your own lamp, and *you* keep that lamp burning."

I looked into his eyes, shocked to be hit with such a deep thought in the middle of a Lane Bryant.

"What makes you feel sexy?" he asked, his voice barely louder than a whisper.

I flatlined. There wasn't a single moment I could remember. There'd been times I'd felt pretty, like when I'd gone out for girls' nights or got dressed up for a wedding, but then people would post pictures and I'd realize just how delusional I'd been. Pictures didn't lie.

He pulled me flush against his body and kissed me again. In

between clothing displays in the middle of a mall clothing store. Unlike the night before when it had been passion unleashed, his kiss was equally as commanding but soft. Like he wanted to make sure every single nerve on both my upper and lower lip knew exactly who was nudging them to attention from their peaceful slumber.

"I'll be right back. I think you have enough in the dressing room to keep you busy for a few minutes."

Surrounded by the dozens of outfits we'd selected for me to try on, I could finally catch my breath and reorient myself. I felt off my axis. Like I'd been cruising for years and finally landed back on *terra firma* and yet my legs refused to cooperate. My pulse felt like I'd spent hours in a rave trying to keep pace with EDM beats all night long. And my nipples! Jesus, they didn't just poke through my cotton t-shirt. They'd turned into heat seeking missiles jutting out so far and twisted so tight, just removing my cotton t-shirt had me moaning at the delicious ache.

I cycled through a few outfits that were definite *no's*, landing on a pair of stretch pleather pants that had me convinced I was Beyonce in town for a mini-residency. There was a black, shimmery, peek-a-boo shoulder top with a dramatic train that looked so *boss* paired together, it had me nearly convinced I could do this sexy thing that Cash kept talking about.

As if just by thought alone, he softly rapped on my dressing room door.

"One more thing." He tossed something satiny in deep purple over the top.

It was a satin and lace basque with matching panties in a deep amethyst floral. He was smoking crack. There was not enough Crisco in the world to shimmy my ass into that *delicate* lace that needed to meander either all the way up from my hips to my tits or shimmy down from my pits to my bits.

I was afraid to even touch it. To accept the offering that hung from his fingers over the door meant I'd consider it. And I definitely wasn't considering it. There was no way.

"May I come in?"

The door handle jiggled. What possessed me to open the door for him? Maybe I was smoking crack, too. I'm glad I did though, because when he locked eyes with me, those two oceanic orbs were pure smoke and heat. And my lady bits preened.

"Wow. Harlow. That outfit is just."

He cleared his throat and looked in my eyes again. I wished offhand I could get to my cell phone fast enough to snap a picture of the way he looked at me. When the weekend was over, I'd want photographic evidence of that smoldering gaze for future bedtime motivation.

"No one is going to be looking that closely at me." I pointed toward the lingerie still hanging on his finger.

"This is just for you. Your own private shot of self-confidence."

"I don't know how suffocating myself with a flimsy piece of fabric that I'll be worrying all night will tear at the seams will help me feel confident enough to win a poker tournament."

He pulled at his lip. I could see he wanted to say something, but he refrained. Instead he took the lingerie from its delicate hanger and held it out toward me.

"Do me a favor?" he asked. "Just try it on. For me?"

When I didn't make a move, he upped the ante. "Consider it part of the requirements for helping you win your tournament."

He could take his assistance and shove it. I didn't do conditions. Not like that.

"That's okay."

I tried to reach around him to open the door. He caught my wrist, circling my pulse point with his thumb. I swear he had some kind of voodoo magic emitting from his pores because the skin to skin contact sent my entire circulatory system into overdrive.

He raised my wrist to his mouth, placing a kiss right at my pulse point. There was no doubt he could feel the hummingbird patter of the blood in my veins. I may have moaned.

"Whether just for tonight, or if it impacts how you feel for the rest of your life, you're gorgeous. Sexy. Sinful."

He separated each word with another kiss on my wrist. His compliments were like raindrops hitting an ocean. The words felt nice for the moment they glanced the surface but disappeared into the wide expanse of self -doubt.

"You need to feel it, Harlow. *You* need to be radiating it. Believing it."

Somehow the outfit transferred from his hands to mine. In the span of time it took my brain to catch up, Cash was already out the door of the dressing room. I stood there, speechless, with my missile nipples, my hummingbird pulse, and some come fuck me lingerie that he convinced me to try on with nothing more than a kiss on the wrist.

CHAPTER 9

CASH 

I t was just supposed to be a quick trip to buy an outfit. That was it. To give her something that she felt cute and flirty in that would make her smile and toss her hair all night and distract all the assholes with too much bravado into bleeding out their pots.

Somehow it had become an exercise in getting her to see herself like I did. Why was that suddenly so important to me? She was a blip. In the grand scheme of things this trip to Vegas was nothing. An excuse to get together with my brothers. By next year this time, I'd more than likely forget her soulful eyes, or her pouty mouth that hid the most bewitching smile. Or the way she threw her whole head into her laughter and wrinkled her nose while she did it. And then she went and put on leather fucking leggings that traced every ridge of her muscular calves and that apple of an ass, and I wanted to press her up against the dressing room mirror and let her *feel* for herself my opinion of her in those pants.

Presley: Harris doesn't think before he opens his stupid mouth

Presley: He didn't mean what he said.

Of course, my brothers would hone in on the euphoria I floated on.

Me: Not a big deal.

I didn't want to engage in any more conversations about my childhood trauma. Especially with two assholes who were *hair of the dog*-ing it and didn't have control of their mouths.

Presley: I'm really sorry his dumb mouth fucked up a great morning

Presley: Please come back. We're gonna go to Top Golf.

Me: You guys go ahead. Harlow asked for my help. So I'll catch up with you guys later.

Presley: 😮

Presley: What is it about Las Vegas and Murrays?

"Alright, let's go."

Harlow had her shopping bag pressed to her side like it contained nuclear codes.

"Shoes?" I asked.

"I'm sure I can make do with what I have back at the hotel."

"Somehow I'm unconvinced you have any shoe that goes with leather pants."

After convincing Harlow that she did in fact need a pair of fuck me boots to complete the outfit, we made our way back to the hotel so we could go over the basics of poker psychology. We covered spotting someone's tell and paying attention to face cards during each round. While not super important, having a mental tally of face cards that had been played would give her an edge when trying to figure out how good an opponent's hand was in later rounds.

"You check your cards too often when you have a good hand." I told her after a few rounds of play. "Even when you have something as inconsequential as a pair of pocket twos. When you're playing, either check your cards after each card reveals whether you have a good hand or not; or remind yourself not to look at them more than once."

"There's too much shit to remember!" She ran a frustrated hand through her hair, tossing it over her shoulder.

"And definitely do a lot of that."

"More of what?"

"Teasing me with that mane of spun silk you call hair. Every time you toss your hair *I* forget what cards I have."

Her mouth twisted as if I'd told her she smelled like moldy cheese.

"I'm hot and uncomfortable. I seriously think I'm pitting out!" She raised her arms, flapping the cotton of her t-shirt. "Teasing you wasn't anywhere near the top ten of things going on in my brain right now."

"You flirt without even realizing you're doing it."

Addictive. That's what she was. She snorted a derisive laugh.

"Considering the reason I *won* this trip to Vegas was because I am, in fact, the *worst* flirt in all of Chicago, apparently, I'd say flirting is definitely nowhere in the orbit of my talents and abilities. I proved it. In spades. On the radio."

I couldn't take it anymore. I'd politely tolerated the pot shots she took at herself all morning while we shopped. She wasn't mine. I didn't have the right to call her on her bullshit. But I saw it. I saw through what she was doing.

Rounding the table, I extended my hand to her without saying a word. She took it, a question mark in her quirked eyebrow. I pulled her close, and she came right to me, her hands settling on my waist, and the moss color of her eyes deepening to forest.

My fingers itched with need to feel the silk of the hair I'd just been pining to feel. I cupped her jaw, traced a path from her lips to her ear with my mouth.

"You are charming." I kissed her jaw just below her ear and luxuriated in her shiver, "Desirable and addictive. I watch how men watch you. The heat in their stares. They feel it just like I do. Your magnetism. It feels like sunshine and sin."

She pulled away squaring me with a look of disbelief, determined to find the bullshit residing there. Rather than try to convince her with words, I dove in, attacking her mouth in an attempt to remove any doubt from forming on her lips. They were sinful. Every time I kissed her, I felt untethered.

"Somewhere in your foundation is a crack," I told her, hoping she could see the honesty in my face, hear it in my voice. "It tells you that you aren't worthy of male attention. That somehow it's *wrong* for them to desire you. Because that's what society has told you. That's not an inability to flirt. It's a lack of realization that you are just as worthy as any other woman. Just because you don't believe a man is capable of flirting with you or desiring you, doesn't negate the fact that they do and they are."

There was no time left, the tournament began in a few short hours. I could only hope my words took root. And that she would be surrounded by a bunch of idiots with more bravado than skill.

"Are you sure about this, Murray? If Dino catches wind..."

I had friends at most of the casinos. Krew, Aria's pit boss, was no different.

"Dino doesn't give a shit about unsponsored shoot outs. He wants his paws on the national, big pot tourneys. Besides, Dino and I *came to an understanding* years ago."

"I don't know..."

I'm sure he said more, but already I'd lost interest in the discussion. Harlow and her sister approached the check in area. She wore the leathery pants and that shimmery one shouldered blouse like they owed her something. It had my mouth watering with desperation to kiss that naked shoulder and run my nose up her neck. In it, she somehow looked demure and ripe with sexuality simultaneously. But the boots. The ones I insisted she buy? Tawdry thoughts of lifting her up and splaying her across the poker table with those heels on my shoulders were on rapid repeat behind my eyelids.

If the outfit hadn't already stiffened my cock to discomfort, her hair and makeup unlocked a new level. She was ... some kind of word that hadn't yet been invented yet since none of the ones in my vocabulary seemed appropriate. What a terrible injustice. Not a single phrase in the American dictionary accurately described the sweet sin that walked toward me.

Her hair fell in bouncy curls down her shoulders, seductively framing the breasts hidden behind her demure shirt. She had a few strands pinned away from her face, old Hollywood movie star, style. Her makeup? Fuck me with those too-long-to-be-real lashes and that ruby red, took a bite straight from Eve's apple, lipstick.

I wasn't in control of my own body. My feet floated toward

her *Exorcist* style, to where she and her sister stood. I was hypnotized.

"You'll need to check your cell phone in with the table to your right." The hotel staff member told Harlow as he handed her the player's packet. "No texting, filming, pictures, or live streaming during the event. At the end of each round, you will have a fifteen-minute break to stand, get some water, and use the facilities in the roped off section. Those fifteen minutes are firm. If you miss the start, you will be eliminated from the tournament and you will have to buy back in. You can only do so once. Once the second day of tournament play begins, no more buy-ins are allowed. Buy-Ins double each round."

She looked like a lost puppy walking down a busy street in New York City. She continued to accept the pieces of paper he handed over to her and signed where he told her to sign. From her glossy, wide-eyed stare, there was no way she digested everything he had to say.

"Cash Murray?" The staff member's voice went up at the end, barely hiding his surprise. "Are you playing in *this* tournament?"

I'd been walking around the damn casino for two full days and not a soul recognized me. Suddenly I pin a number to the pocket of my jacket and the press releases get sent out. Typical.

"Harlow," I ignored the guy still ogling at me, and directed my focus to the woman I'd been desperate to see all day. "There isn't a word that feels appropriate with how stunning you look."

She glanced at me from beneath her eyelashes, a flush pinkening her already made-up cheeks.

"You must be Cash. I'm Harlow's sister, Lennox."

The two were no doubt sisters. They had the same moss-colored eyes and sweet button noses. However, that was where their similarities in looks diverged. Seeing her stand next to her sister, I understood with perfect clarity why Harlow felt so self-conscious. Her sister definitely had a beauty queen aura about her. Perfectly styled hair just a shade darker than Harlow's, a very shapely figure on full display in her nothing-to-the-imagination strapless dress, which was being held up by a set of hard-to-miss, very firm and perky breasts. I'm sure thousands of men found her gorgeous. I just wasn't one of them.

"Can you believe this?" She gestured to the tournament. "I'm so worried that Lo is in over her head! Don't get me wrong, I love that you're doing this for me," she turned her head and looked back at her sister, "but I'm a ball of anxiety right now."

Lo. An interesting nickname. I much preferred Harlow. It was intoxicatingly elegant.

"She's going to do great. The best position to be in, when in a situation like this, is underestimated."

I ran my hand down Harlow's back, pulling her into an awkward side hug that had her sister's eyes widening. Harlow looked up at me with a twinkle in her eye that made me feel like I provided her the air she breathed.

Our little exchange of pleasantries got cut off. The announcer of the tournament told everyone to make their way to their tables so the tournament could begin.

"Cash!" Presley waved at me from the throughway between the poker tables and the buffet. "What the hell are you doing?"

Fuck. This was the absolute last thing I needed to be dealing with. Harlow smiled at me and waved, passing through the velvet rope and walking toward her table. I lost my chance to give her a last minute pep talk. To kiss her for good luck. To whisper in her ear how sexy I thought she was and how I knew the men that sat at the table she approached didn't know what was coming for them. Instead, I got to spend that time having a directionless conversation with my brother.

"I thought you said you were spending the day with the girl?"

Presley was taller than I was, by easily five inches. At that moment, with his mulishly set jaw and ire spiking in his amber colored eyes, I felt a full foot shorter than him.

"She's right there."

I pointed over my shoulder toward where she sat smiling and

chatting with one of the guys at her table, tossing her hair over her shoulder as she adjusted in her seat and got comfortable.

"You said you weren't gonna gamble."

"I'm not."

I turned looking once again toward the tournament. The countdown clock read five minutes and eleven seconds. I couldn't DQ right out of the gate otherwise I had no way of keeping tabs on how Harlow was faring.

I felt him pull at the number on my lapel pocket.

"And you just randomly walk around the casino in Cash the Hustler attire with numbers hanging from your pocket?"

I caught the soft tremble in his voice. He sounded hurt, like I'd told some egregious lie. Which I hadn't. Not technically.

And I always wore a sports coat. Not just when I played poker. The only difference was the sunglasses. And the number hanging from my pocket that said I now had four minutes and two seconds to get to my seat.

"Pres, I can't explain now. Harlow needed my help. I'm helping her. That's all. I still hate Vegas. I still hate Atlantic City. I don't want to be part of this scene anymore. Nothing has changed. I just really need to get to my table."

I turned and shot off behind the ropes without looking back. I knew what I'd see if I looked at Presley. Even without physically seeing it, I imagined what he looked like standing there. Disappointed. Shocked. Sad. If I honestly had decided to come back to this lifestyle, I'd be upset, too. But I wasn't. I just wanted to protect Harlow.

CHAPTER 10

Harlow

felt like I was going to throw up. What on earth possessed me to do such a stupid thing? I barely knew anything about poker. Here I was in a tournament, blinded by some altruistic desire to help my sister, and certain I'd fall right on my ass in the first round.

Cash sat across from me at the same table. I didn't remember seeing his name on the screen earlier. He certainly never mentioned it, not even once all morning while we shopped.

I felt him looking at me. Everywhere. My skin tingled like the beginnings of a sunburn. Hot, prickly, as if the only thing that could provide relief would be a naked dive into a pool of ice-cold water. And we already know where I stood on skinny dipping with Cash. Yes, please.

Lennox had turned me into Poker Player Barbie, with big curly hair and fake over the top eyelashes. Despite all of the protestations I'd voiced, I felt hot. Like model hot. I didn't care if my belly was being held in with spandex, and that without this super restrictive fake leather, my thighs would jiggle. In the here and now? I felt like a Kardashian.

Despite his eyes being hidden behind a set of mirrored sunglasses, I could see my reflection in them. He was ogling me. In fact, he hadn't taken his eyes off of me since we sat down. I'd purchased the stupid lingerie he suggested I wear. The deepest color amethyst with the most beautiful floral pattern. It held me tight in all the right places and cradled and pushed up the girls to where they were offered up by the softest satin. And damn, if he hadn't been right about lingerie providing another level of self-confidence.

I had a hard time concentrating with him so intently focused on me. I tried to stick to what he'd told me. Every time the dealer put a new card down, I glanced at mine. My hair had been tossed over my shoulder so many times, show ponies would be envious. Though I had no way of guessing whether it looked sexy or awkward.

I knew at least one person couldn't stop staring at me. Every call, raise, fold, he stared me down. I became so wrapped up in his intense focus on me, that I barely noticed our first player at the table to be eliminated. When that happened, they called our first fifteen-minute break.

"God, watching you play is torture," Cash whispered in my ear.

I stood waiting for the restroom, worried I wouldn't get back before fifteen minutes was called. He appeared practically out of nowhere at my side. The sunglasses he'd worn through the whole round rested on his head. He regarded me with such intense attention, every single nerve cell that slept during my sexual hiatus unspooled and stretched into awareness.

"You have every man at that table wrapped around your finger, and you don't even realize it," he continued, playing with a ringlet of my hair.

He was smoking something. The room overflowed with gorgeous women. Gorgeous, thin women who tended to be the standard preference. Common sense said that there was absolutely no way that the seven other people sitting at our table all had eyes for the chubby chick in the pleather leggings. It just wasn't mathematically feasible.

The closer he pressed toward me though, the less I cared. Whatever words he said became white nose to the overwhelming need to feel his lips on me again. It was the least opportune moment for my libido to suddenly become so demanding. But those ocean eyes had me lost in a sea of desire that he'd created.

"Those lips. Redder than Eve's apple and just as tempting." He rested his forehead against mine. I could feel the struggle in the sexy vibration of his voice. The one that felt like I had a vibrator in my pants egging me on to grab him by his lapels and take what I needed from him.

His fingers traced along my neck, and my pulse skittered. I could barely breathe with the rapid staccato my heart pumped out. His cologne was so subtle, practically undetectable unless one stood as close as I did. Over the smell of cigarettes in the casino, the white, scentless air purifier smell they used to drown out the ever-present cigarette smell, there was him. Like cloves and oranges. It wasn't a combination I could pinpoint to a specific, familiar name brand cologne, but whatever he wore I wanted to own stock in it. There was a five o'clock shadow growing along his jawline. I craved the rough abrasion against my cheek combined with the scent of him. Who was I kidding? I wanted to rub myself all over him like a cat in heat. Because that is exactly how I felt. Strung out with a desperate need to feel possessed by him with much more than just a kiss.

"Just one. For luck."

I had no time to ask what *one* he spoke of. His lips fused against mine, his hand cupping my jaw, holding me in place as I careened down the rabbit hole of longing. I felt untethered, floating, and falling simultaneously. I wanted to both pull away and push against him harder. To run my hands along his chest, down to his hips, and press myself against what I hoped waited for me there.

One kiss turned into a solid five minutes of pressed bodies and soft moans, hidden in the bathroom hallway.

Ladies and Gentleman, five minutes remain.

If not for the overhead announcer, there was no telling just how far that kiss would have gone.

"I messed up your lipstick." He smiled, brushing his thumb along my lip line. "You'll probably need to attend to that."

He kissed me again. Long and slow before releasing me toward the bathroom. I barely recognized the woman in the mirror. Her eyes shone, her lipstick was everywhere but on her lips, and her cheeks were a shade of bright pink that had nothing to do with makeup. Now to go with the sexy feelings from earlier, I also felt *desired*. And that was even headier.

I mainlined an elixir of that feeling. It did what I needed it to in order for me to get through the next round. Steeled me with confidence. I survived round one. I just needed to make it through five more.

"You did great." Cash fell into step beside me as I walked out of the bathroom. He had to have been waiting just outside the door. "I'm sorry my brother pulled me away before I could give you some last-minute pointers."

"Speaking of..." I stopped to face him, flicking the number badge that hung from his lapel. "I didn't know you were playing."

"I didn't either until this gorgeous siren with soulful eyes texted me and asked for my help."

He ran his hands behind his head, color rising on his cheeks. Cash Cole Murray got embarrassed? No way.

"I wasn't aware you could play poker."

"I dabble," he said, placing his hand on my back and escorting us through the velvet rope.

CHAPTER 11

CASH 

I didn't really talk about the poker playing days to people. Mainly because most of those pots didn't even come to me. They went to my snake of a backer.

"Round two is about to start." I tossed my head in the direction of our table. "We have about two minutes to get our butts back into our seats or be disqualified."

The moment we sat back down, the sunglasses slid into place, and it was go time. New deck meant we started over with the count. Was it technically illegal to count cards? Yes. But that was in games like Blackjack where they played with one deck straight out. Hold 'em employed burn cards (ones the dealer tossed away) to prevent counting. But poker was a game of statistics and probability. Both things I excelled at.

"I don't know what the protocol is," Harlow broke me out of my musings, "but good luck, or break a leg, or whatever the appropriate well wish is."

"You too, Hollywood."

She tilted her head, apparently confused by the nickname. With a name like Harlow, and the old movie star glamor she sported with her hair and makeup—I felt like the nickname fit her like a satiny glove worn by the stars of the era.

"You look like a glamorous movie star."

I pointed out just as the dealer called for quiet and began passing out cards. I didn't miss the blush. Or the smile she tried to hide behind her first pair of cards.

The table felt different. There wasn't the same energy I used to feel at the height of my playing days. Harlow was the only woman at our table, surrounded by a bunch of leering, greasy men that reeked of booze and cigarettes. This wasn't a high stakes game in the slightest. These types of games brought in some new blood and interest for the casinos, but most of the people that played these low-level tournaments were either tourists with too much bravado, or the tried-and-true deep-rooted gamblers. The ones they made movies about. The desperate ones.

They were all so easy to read. One sniffed and wiped at his nose when he had a good hand. Another sat up straight every time he was hoping the dealer would give him a good card to build from. It was a minimal effort to pick them off one by one. I'd been so focused on taking out Harlow's competition that I hadn't even noticed the pile of chips she'd been quietly amassing. She only needed to be one of the last three standing in a table of ten. That would get us into tomorrow's championship round. With five total left at our table, I liked her odds.

Since we'd sat back down, I'd barely glanced in Harlow's direction. Mainly because of the raging hard-on that drove me to distraction. If she looked at me with a silken smile and those cam girl eyelashes and lipstick—I'd probably blow in my pants. Instead, I hyper focused on covering her perimeter. Each exposed weakness from one of our opponents was an opportunity to thin the herd.

"It's to you." Her sweet voice cut through my musings like a raindrop.

Just one problem with that. I'd spent so much time focused on her opponents; I had zero idea of how she'd been playing. Had she shifted game play since this morning? Taken my advice? Buried her tells? Where *was* her weakness now?

The dealer gave me pocket tens. Decent, but nothing to celebrate over. I looked at Harlow, grateful my sunglasses hid my eyes. Rather than look at me, she kept her face down, looking at her cards once again and biting her lip. Had she bitten her lip before? Was that the first time she'd done it? Did she remember what I said to her about repeating an action to not expose a tell?

The only thing my brain wanted to do though was remind me of what that lip felt like. Tasted like. How soft and pliant those lips were against mine. The way she yielded when I pressed into her, softening her spine and rolling her hips to greet me.

"What's his pot?" I pointed toward the greasy looking guy with the sniffing problem.

"Two fifty." The dealer told me.

I easily quadrupled that.

"Call."

I challenged him to his all-in. He rubbed his nose, sniffing again, pushing all his chips into the center. Double bonus it also forced the guy to his left between him and Harlow to also go all-in.

The three cards that made up the flop gave me a potential full house with a third ten hitting. Statistically there were only a few things that could beat my three of a kind. I felt fairly confident I had the hand in the bag. Harlow looked at her cards a second time and checked me, leaving me the option to also check and go with no bet or add more money into the pot.

She wore the sweetest smile. Those full kissable lips taunting me once again. The hair she'd tossed over her shoulder diffused the sweetest smell of spun sugar across the table.

"Call." She added a pittance of chips compared to the mountain she'd attained and placed them gently in the center.

The final cards did nothing for me, but lo and behold the little card shark had pocket Queens, thus taking the table with a full house, and ending the round by knocking out her last two competitors. It was the two of us, and the last guy left at the table, moving on to the championship round.

CHAPTER 12

Harlow

Holy shit. Holy shit on hot buttered toast with a shot of get the motherfucking fuckity fuck out of here. I survived a poker tournament. Well, day one of the tournament. Not just finished, motherfucking won the damn thing. Finished in position one. I couldn't stop celebrating in my head while I stood in complete shock.

Cash stood clapping walking around toward me, but my sister shot in from out of nowhere and yanked me into a hug.

"You won! Holy shit, Lo, you won! You're in the next round!"

"Ladies, the tournament is still going on and you're creating a disturbance."

One of the hotel staff shooed us out of the tournament space and past the velvet ropes. The moment we were standing on the regular casino floor, Cash dove in, stealing me away from my sister.

"You did it!" He beamed, cradling my face between his hands.

One minute I'd been about to excitedly tell him how I couldn't believe it, and he'd been in my head the whole time reminding me not to give away my tells, and the next I was pressed against a hotel beam, acutely aware of a *raise* in the game of *poke her*.

"I want to bend you over that table right there and fuck you till you scream." He rasped into my ear, hiding his tawdry come-on behind a bear hug. "I'd settle for dinner, but by the daggers your sister is shooting me right now, how about you call me when you're done celebrating?"

He kissed me with such blatant hunger that it stole my breath and all reasonable thought, and he took it with him when he strutted away with a smug smile on his face. Guess I'd have to find him later in order to get it back. Oh, the tragedy.

"Umm, is there something you'd like to tell me about?" Lennox looped her arm through mine as we strutted through the casino toward the exit.

My body vibrated with adrenaline and euphoria. Between the shock of winning my round, the air stealing, blatantly sexual kiss from Cash, and the euphoria of knowing both of those things happened to me, I floated down Las Vegas Blvd. Fuck me boots be damned, I couldn't even feel my feet.

"Oh my god, I'm starving. Like I could legit pound a buffet right now." I laughed as we turned south down the strip.

"Maybe just a burger. It's almost nine o'clock. Your metabolism stopped optimally burning calories hours ago."

Count on Lennox to throw a bucket of cold water on my celebratory mood.

"Can you stop being body obsessed for like five minutes and just enjoy the damn moment?"

Lennox huffed, stopping in the middle of the walkway to the great annoyance of what felt like half of Las Vegas.

"I'm an E.R. nurse, Harlow. I can't just shut it off. Do you know what I see more of in the E.R. than anything else? Heart attacks. So, I'm sorry if you don't like that I'm concerned for my health and your health, but that won't stop me from caring."

"Except you're not caring. You're judging. You're suffocating me with your judgment just like Mom used to. For one night, one goddamn night, I just want to feel like a normal person. Doing normal things like celebrating without having you judge me, or mentally count my calories in your head, or the million other ways that you tell me I'm *less than* every motherfucking time I'm with you."

Lennox gaped. I don't think I'd ever clapped back at Lennox that hard before. Had we argued? Of course. We were sisters who were eighteen months apart. Being that close in age made fighting inevitable through every course of our lives. But I'd never stepped up, nose to nose, and full on challenged her.

"I'm going to head back to the hotel," she clipped. "Enjoy your dinner."

Whatever. She could turn tail and run back to the hotel. You know what, I could go back to the hotel too.

> Me: Hey. Dinner fell through. You busy?

> Cash: My brothers and I are at The Henry over in the Cosmopolitan. Join us 🩶

He texted me a heart. I tried not to read into that. It was just a thing. Something people did to show you were welcome and not encroaching. And men didn't pay attention to the heart color thing. So what if it was a red heart. It meant nothing.

He stood at the front door to the casino, hands in his pockets, scanning the crowds as I approached. The moment he saw me, he held his hand out with a smile.

"Wow, and the boots are still on! I thought for sure you'd be back in your flip flops by now."

He squeezed my hand and turned toward the restaurant.

"Guys, this is Harlow. Harlow, my younger brothers, Presley and Harris. Harris, you might remember meeting briefly last night."

While they each had distinct features all their own—Cash had the darkest hair of the three of them—there was absolutely no doubt they were all brothers.

"My other younger brother flew back to San Diego last night to propose to his girlfriend. But he'll be back in the morning," Cash explained, pulling a chair out for me.

"Wait, he's *proposing?*" Harris, the one I'd met yesterday, looked at Cash utterly gobsmacked.

"Are you kidding me?" Presley tossed his phone on the table, massaging his temples. "What part of 'I had an urgent question I had to ask her, so I *borrowed a billion dollar plane from ESPN and flew the red eye back to San Diego'* didn't clue you in to that fact? What important question did you think he was asking her? Whether they should live in North City or Del Mar?"

Harris shrugged with a mischievous smile that was so similar to Cash's.

"I wasn't really paying attention to much of anything this morning. I figured if it was something important someone would fill me in."

"Where's your sister?" Cash asked me, putting his arm around my shoulder.

I rolled my eyes in response. "Long story. Don't ask."

"Oh, so it looks like we all are annoyed with our siblings today," Presley chirped, looking straight at Cash when he did.

What the hell had I just stepped into?

CHAPTER 13

CASH 

nviting Harlow to dinner was exactly the buffer I needed. After the tournament ended, I knew I needed to face the music with Presley. As badly as I'd wanted to hang out with Harlow, all the ignored text messages showed in an angry stream on my phone when I went to collect it.

Presley: How could you?

Presley: You promised all of us you were done with gambling

Presley: Did you not learn your lesson?

Presley: You said that you couldn't gamble in Vegas anymore.

Presley: That was the deal to get Dino off your back.

Presley: So why the fuck are you dragging around a bloodied corpse waiting for the lion to come and find you eating a kill on his turf?

> Presley: Mom and Dad are going to be so disappointed when they find out

> Cash: Come meet me for dinner. We'll talk. Let's go to The Henry. I like it there. It's quiet.

Both of them met me. Harris wore his usual give no shits face, just glad to be part of the group. Presley, on the other hand, had years of practice replicating the judgmental and disappointed face of my father.

"I just don't understand, Cash," He said as he slid into the booth. "You said coming to Vegas would be okay. That you weren't addicted to gambling. That you'd be able to stay away from the tables. You said they made you sick. Physically sick."

He was right. They did. I wasn't a gambler as he thought I was. I didn't have an addiction. I'd become a poker player because I didn't want a desk job. When I graduated college I wasn't down for signing my life away to a nine to five that would turn into a seven thirty to seven thirty, where I'd be choked by ties every day of my damn life and pretend to have a social life on weekends golfing with my buddies. I wanted to travel. To see the world. To be free like Beckett was. That kid had more stamps on his passport than a pilot.

Playing poker made me sick because it was a constant reminder of all I'd lost being stupid and ill informed. How in the naivete of a twenty-two year old, I'd happily signed on Dino's dotted line. So grateful to have someone think I was good enough to be in the professional circuit. Thrilled I had an *agent* to look out for me. To guide me, and make sure I played in the best tournaments in the world.

I never would have suspected that backing came with a

hundred and twenty percent buy back. With each game they staked, I dug my own financial grave. By the time I was thirty, I was chained to Dino with diamond encrusted anvils with no hope of ever getting free. Until someone finally clued me in to what predatory staking was. And Dino Frangioni was the king of predatory stakes.

I quietly played online tournaments. Slowly building a fortune on the side, under a different unknown name. Gaining notoriety in the online world just as I did in live tournaments, until I'd squirreled away enough money to buy my freedom. Of course, that didn't go over too well with Dino. If I bought myself out, to the tune of almost five hundred thousand dollars, he wouldn't have his favorite familiar to suck the life blood from.

He filed a complaint with the gaming commission that I had illegally played unbacked tournaments on the side in violation of my contract with him. My dad lawyered me up with expensive New York City lawyers who were well versed in Dino's kind. Dino begrudgingly released me from my contract, under the condition that I never play a staked tournament in Vegas again.

Which was why I fled to Atlantic City and played in the lower circuits: Reno, Henderson, Laughlin, and a few places along the gulf. But after a few years of doing that I just wasn't interested anymore. So now, I floated, rudderless, in search of purpose. Beckett kept trying to convince me to move to San Diego. Living on the opposite coast didn't exactly appeal to me, but at least I'd be by him. I just wanted a quiet life somewhere.

"Presley, please don't turn this into an After School Special. I promise, hand to God, I don't have a gambling problem. Harlow and I met yesterday at the bar. We hung out for a bit before Beckett sent Harris to come and collect me. After he bailed and I lost the two of you in the crowd, I bumped into her at Caesars. Her sister called in a panic over some kind of I don't know financial issue, and today, Harlow texted me that she'd decided to buy into a poker tournament in some altruistic attempt to help out her sister. That's all."

"Except Pres saw you playing Cash. You're not supposed to be playing. At all."

"Jesus. Dino doesn't care about some no name, insignificant game put on by the hotel. He cares about the WSOP million-dollar pots with sponsorship opportunities and extended tv contracts and payouts."

He lost his cash cow. That's what he's pissed about. He wants me back so he can fuck me over with a shit contract and steal all my money.

Harlow's text couldn't have come at a more perfect time. The last thing I wanted to do was go three or four rounds with the two of them. They said their peace. It was heard loud and clear. But there was no point belaboring it.

At least with her presence the two of them resorted back to the genial, entertaining goof balls they usually were when not trying to pull the concerned brothers card.

Harlow still wore the outfit she'd competed in. The moment I saw her sashay up the walkway to the hotel, I felt just as twisted with desire as I had seeing her for the first time. I wanted to cart her off to my hotel room and steal away for hours—not sleeping.

"So why are your brothers annoyed with you?" she asked, catching up to the conversation.

"I'll tell you later." I nuzzled her cheek, whispering in her ear.

"I hear you're quite the card shark." Presley volleyed.

Harlow shrugged, hiding her smile behind the menu she studied intently.

"Honestly, it's beginner's luck. The only poker I play live is with my family during the holidays for quarters. Yesterday seriously was the very first time I've sat down at a table and played for real. Besides, if it wasn't for this one here..." she snaked her arm through mine and leaned into me as if we were dating. Like I was the most important person sitting at that table. "...I probably wouldn't have even made it out of the first round!"

She looked up at me with those moss-colored eyes, presently lined in sin and smoke, and beamed so brightly in my direction I would have sworn she was phosphorescent. I didn't want to eat dinner anymore. Being with my brothers suddenly seemed like the lesser of the two options. I wanted her to hop on my back so we could run across the street, bulldoze into my room, and spend the next twelve hours working up an even greater appetite.

"You mentioned your brother and a jet?" she asked, nodding a thanks to the waitress who set down a glass of sparkling water.

"He *borrowed* ESPN's jet to fly back to San Diego last night. So he could propose to his girlfriend."

"Driving wasn't an option?" she asked with a smirk.

"When Beckett wants something, he pursues it with mulish focus. Nothing can distract him."

She nodded, twirling a strand of her hair around her fingers, looking at me with mischief lighting her eyes.

"Sounds like you and Beckett have a lot in comm— wait a second. Beckett. Your brother, Beckett...Murray? Beckett Murray is your brother?"

"Technically, he's *all* of our brothers." Harris clarified with a wink.

"The Olympian?"

"Former, but yes." I took her hand in mine, swiping my lips across her knuckles, drinking in her shiver like it was my lifeblood.

"The one who peed in the fountain?"

"Not his best moment, but I'd suggest if you meet him tomorrow not opening with that one," I chuckled. "He's working really hard to overcome that and move past it."

"You're Beckett Murray's *brother*," she said again.

"Yes, we've established that." I laughed. "He's the swimmer, I play poker, Presley swims and coaches for the Big 12, and Harris started a company to teach little kids how not to be afraid of the ocean. So swimming kind of runs in the family. Except me. But I guess you could say I swim with the sharks."

I waggle my eyebrows in her direction, hoping for a laugh.

"So not just a dabble then?" she asked with a chagrined smile.

I shrug. "Not a dabble."

"He's a WSOP champion." Harris tells her. "Like ten or twelve really big tournaments. I'm surprised he hasn't been recognized."

His voice dropped on the last line. I knew that wasn't a compliment. He meant that he was surprised Dino hadn't caught wind that I'd been playing.

"I'm not wearing my glasses," I tell Harris, pulling them from my pocket. "But I'm a washed up, has been. I promise you no one gives a shit that I'm playing."

"No one gives a shit until they do," Harris says, voice strained.

I don't know what Presley and Harris thought Dino would do to me if he found out I was playing in a tournament. This wasn't *Casino*. It's not like Dino had the power to abduct me and leave me in the desert buried up to my neck and wait for the creatures to have their way with me. He was a no one, too. Some overblown cocksucker who wielded power to the powerless. I wasn't powerless, and he knew it.

"Harris, seriously, not a single person in Las Vegas cares that I'm here."

"I do." Harlow ran her fingers through my hair, smiling up at me when I turned to look at her.

"And you're the only one who matters, Hollywood."

CHAPTER 14

Harlow

wasn't ready to go back to my room. The last person I wanted to spend any time with was my judgmental sister.

The longer I spent away, the more justified I felt. All of this ridiculousness was for her. So that she didn't have to worry about keeping a roof over their heads.

"Usually at this point in the date someone would say 'want to come back to my place and hang out or talk or whatever?'"

Cash laced his fingers through mine as we walked across the street back to the hotel.

"And both parties know it's code for let's go to my place and have sex. But they dance around each other until they feel comfortable and then they bang. Since we're both staying at the same hotel, if I ask you to my room, there's not really much dancing around the subject since it's just a bed up there."

He rubbed the back of his neck, a flush creeping up over the collar of his shirt. It charmed me that he was as awkwardly embarrassed as I was. I'd never been the one-night stand type. I was a serial monogamist, and if being totally honest, I'd only had two boyfriends.

I wanted to go up to his room, though. Despite knowing that what we had more than likely would fade when we returned to our normal lives, my whole body screamed *Carpe Diem!* Well, except it was nighttime. Technically we'd be seizing the night, but I digress.

We stood at the elevator banks. His finger hovered over the up button. It was surprisingly empty given it wasn't even ten o'clock. Just one heated stare from Cash's deep blue eyes and electricity zipped up and down my spine.

"Do you want to come up to my room and fuck me?" Cash asked, leaning in and taking ownership of my lips. "Because the only thing I've been thinking about since yesterday is getting you spread on my bed, hooking those boots over my shoulders, and making the rest of the fourteenth floor really damn jealous when they hear you moaning my name for the next three hours."

I didn't know if it was his bravado that called to me, or the awkwardness it hid. But where the come -ons made me blush, they also made me want to bend and agree to whatever he offered up.

I could only nod, pulling my lip between my teeth as I pressed the up button.

"Tell me," he said, pulling at my lip before guiding my face toward his own.

I gasped at the sensation of his teeth taking a firm little nibble across the very lip I'd just been worrying. If the elevator didn't arrive soon, we'd give the security surveillance quite the show.

"Say it."

He brushed my hair off my shoulders, taking a hold of it and gently directing my gaze up to his, "Tell me, 'Cash I want you to take me up to your room and make me scream.'"

I felt the heat from my hair follicles down to my toes. I'd never said anything so overtly sexual in my entire life. I didn't think I could.

"Tell me, or the next thing I insist you say is 'Please Cash, bend me over your bed and fuck me til I'm screaming.' Having you flirt and tease all day long, Hollywood, has me hard and desperate."

The elevator dinged and we stepped in. The moment the doors closed, Cash caged me in, holding my hand against his chest.

"I'm trying to be a gentleman." He kissed me on the tip of my nose. "But since every time I say something a little naughty and sexually suggestive, your pupils blow out the color of your irises, I think you like being brought to the edge of propriety and told to spit over it."

He still had my hand cupped in his, which he moved down to the front of his pants, tracing over the bulge that left little doubt how into this exchange he was.

The elevator dinged and announced we'd made it to the fourteenth floor. I was breathless and panting, and it had nothing to do with traversing the long winding halls of the hotel.

At 1414 Cash stopped, waved his key in front of the door reader, waiting for it to chirp and unlock. Once inside, the door sighed closed and the sound of it clicking shut felt like a shotgun at the start of a marathon. I never thought I'd be the kind of girl to be a tornado of kisses, and sighs, and clothes coming off in every which way. I definitely never thought I'd be agile enough to be a giggle and stumble to the bed person. But everything between Cash and I felt new and undiscovered, yet holistically perfect.

The room was the spitting image of mine. With the exception of his one king to my queens. Even the bathroom was in the same location. Which meant peeling out of my shoes, while trying to maintain some kind of physical contact with Cash, and not kill myself traversing a foreign room nearly blind ended up being quite successful.

"Aww, I wanted to feel those heels on my back while I worshipped your pussy like a man on death row."

His words felt like nuclear rain, dripping onto my skin and searing into my marrow. This heat, the desperate need to be touched, was a total departure from normality. Men didn't come on to me with tawdry words. They didn't make their desire so obvious and overt. I almost convinced myself that it couldn't be real.

"Guess you should have thought about that before you pressed me up against the wall and told me to strip."

I dropped the shoes with a soft thump onto the plush carpet. He crawled over me like a cat in heat. Pressing his body against mine as he climbed up from the foot of the bed. He'd managed to get his shoes off and his pants unbuckled, the bulge of his cock protruding from between the gaping zipper.

"These next."

He took hold of my leather- *like* leggings and yanked. Nearly managing to get them all the way off with one vicious snap of his wrist.

"Fuck. Hollywood. You're the very best wet dream."

The leggings were still at my ankles, binding my legs from moving anywhere. Cash fell forward between my legs, his lips and tongue appreciating the purple floral satin panties I'd purchased upon his suggestion.

"You did this for me?" He pushed my top up, revealing the matching purple basque.

"I did it for me," I replied. "Someone suggested that feeling sexy was a personal thing, and lingerie was the very best confidence booster. So, I bought myself a shot of confidence."

"I approve, Hollywood. I approve very, very much. If you were mine, I'd approve an entire wardrobe's worth of self confidence in every fucking color of the rainbow."

He stood, shucking his pants first, palming his dick through his boxer briefs, before yanking my leggings off my legs and tossing them to the chair in the corner of the room.

"Now the top. I want to see the whole picture."

I pulled my top over my head, leaning against the pillows of his bed, fighting against every instinct that begged me to cover up, and instead feeling the heady power of the hunger of Cash's stare.

He made a circular motion with his finger, the universal sign to turn over.

"Show me the back."

I flipped over, burying my face in the pillow as he appreciated the criss cross backing, set in floral lace, that gathered in a ribbon just above the top of the cheeky panties that cradled my ass and parted it into two firm, perky globes.

"This." His voice rumbled with the gravel of a rock band front man as he ran his hands up and down the satin. "Harlow, you make me hard and achy."

His firm grip landed on each of my cheeks, pressing the tension from the tops of my thighs, and spreading bolts of electricity straight to my clit. I throbbed, desperate for stimulation that would relieve the pulse between my legs.

"Cash."

It sounded like a whine.

"One minute. I'm making a list of all the ways I want to make sure I get to fuck you. Because if I can't appreciate, caress, spank, and worship this ass tonight, I want to ensure I can do it tomorrow."

CHAPTER 15

CASH 

She'd worn my lingerie. By "my" I meant, of course, the one I picked out. The entire night she'd looked confident and sexy and so incredibly addictive, and the whole time she'd been wearing something I picked out.

"Tell me something, Hollywood." I couldn't stop running my hands over the soft fabric and feel the firm expanse of her apple butt. "Did you think about me every time you moved and this soft satin caressed your most private regions?"

I squared my hips to hers, pressing my cock between her cheeks and running it up and down the expanse of that sensuous crack. I nipped at her neck like a wolf in heat, my fingers tangled with hers. I wanted to press myself into her skin, to insinuate myself into every crevice so that when she woke up in the morning, the only thing she would smell was a combination of the two of us.

I rolled that fabric down and off her rear end, biting the juiciest apple of her cheek on my descent. She squealed and tried to kick her leg out to dislodge me from her back. All it did though, was expose the pinkest part of her to my gaze.

"Look at how pretty you are here."

My finger stroked her silken folds, tickling through the hair there.

"Turn over," I whispered, pressing a finger through her wet heat, and finding her throbbing little nub soaked and needy.

"What floor are you staying on?" I asked her.

Confusion danced across her face, morphing into panic.

"On eighteen," she told me, trying to press her thighs together and roll off the bed.

I pressed her back into the pillows with one hand, while spreading her open with the other.

"I just wanted to make sure you knew what your goal was."

"M-my goal?" Her voice, both breathy and raspy concurrently, did little to hide the confusion.

"Yes. Your sister is fast asleep on the eighteenth floor. I'm about to make sure you wake her the fuck up, so she knows who's between your thighs worshipping you like the goddess you are."

I didn't give her a second to react to what I said. I ducked down and suffocated myself on her delicious heat. I wanted to be everywhere all at once. Every lick she mewled like a needy kitten. Each suckle on her distended little nub had her hips flying off the bed and my name falling from her lips. When I pressed my fingers into her depths in search of her g-spot her moans and cries became nonsensical, telling me it was too much and also felt so good—concurrently.

"Cash," she elongated the *sh* like a snake shaking its rattle. She thrust her hips up to meet my searching fingers, pressing herself against the pads of my fingers buried deep inside her.

"Tell me, gorgeous, what do you need?"

"More." She panted, unabashedly fucking my fingers.

Watching her take her own pleasure twisted my insides. I wanted to burrow into her depths and camp out there for the rest of our vacation. My mind played an infinite reel of the various ways I wanted to take her. To rut into her like a dog in heat, to slide in slowly, watching her mouth go slack and her pupils devour that mossy green I'd become addicted to. I wanted to force her into her boots, stand her up, and fuck her against the wall, feeling those pointy tips press into my ass as I took her over the edge. And, this tiny kernel of my soul that kept throbbing enough to distract me from my goal. It wanted me to lay her out and make slow, sweet love to her. Those thoughts...I didn't even want to entertain those. Thoughts like those were a result of too long of a sexual hiatus. A couple of heated kisses and some flirting, and suddenly I wanted to create an unbreakable vow with her. Not happening.

"Alright, Hollywood, I'm about to light you up."

CHAPTER 16

Harlow

reathless. Boneless. Swirling with white hot need. I felt too many things all at once. I'd only ever had one person go down on me, and let's just say it hadn't been the most enjoyable experience. Cash didn't just go down on me, he worshipped my pussy. He'd licked, sucked, caressed, impaled, and stimulated every square inch and returned for more.

"I'm about to light you up."

The weighted promise sent a shiver through me. He delivered. With his fingers still twisting inside of me, reducing me to a moaning, needy mess, his mouth fused onto my clit and sucked as if he intended to remove my soul through that turgid piece of my anatomy.

The orgasm hit like a tidal wave. Crashing into me with such force, I was powerless to its pull. The sensations were so intense, the pleasure so all-consuming, the only thing I *could* do was moan as every muscle in my body clamped down and released on the headiest flood of pleasure I'd ever felt.

It seemed like an eternity before conscious thought rejoined my body. Cash stood over me, rolling on a condom, drinking me in with a heated stare.

"You brought condoms with you to Vegas?" I asked when my mouth felt capable of functioning again. "Aren't you the confident one."

"I bought them this afternoon in the hotel gift shop." He watched me watching him. Damn if it wasn't the most erotic thing I'd experienced. "And think of it more as putting my intentions into the universe. Less assuming I'd have you in my bed."

He climbed over me once again, his lips trailing seductive trails up my arm, across my collarbone, and down to the breasts that called to him, begging for his attention. He slid inside me and my world went hazy. Rather than the demanding, animalistic need he'd teased and manipulated earlier, this was a meandering path to fulfillment. As if we hiked a trail and rather than making the summit the destination, we stopped and admired each flower, butterfly, and plant on the way.

It was the most pleasurable give and take. Not only loving the sensations that Cash elicited from my own body, but similarly finding ways to make him groan, flex, swear, and moan.

"Mmm, Harlow." His voice turned into the soft gravel of an eighties hair band front man, as he sang my name with each slow push into me. "The dream was nothing like reality."

His mouth was my drug. Whether he kissed my lips or my body, the warm heat of his mouth sent my pulse into overdrive, intoxicating me with the headiest combination of desire and need. As I toed dangerously close to my own conclusion, I tried to promise myself we'd do this again. And I'd ask him to use his lips everywhere he'd missed. My neck, my back. I wanted to feel his mouth clamp down on my shoulder as he took me from behind, bent over the bed. I wanted to fuck him in the shower, or hell, while skinny dipping in the pool. Damn the consequences.

"Cash," I clawed at his back, trying to force him deeper, press him harder, to control the speed and pressure with which he pushed inside of me. "I need it."

I didn't recognize my voice. It hung in the air, thick with the tendrils of desire I felt zipping through my bloodstream. Was it possible for body and soul to separate while still alive? Because without a doubt, I was convinced I just had the most intense out of body experience. I observed our coupling from the ceiling, looking down at the pornographic scene spread out below me. Awed by how sensual and sexual the moment was.

"I know, Hollywood, but it will be so much better this way." He sucked at my pulse point, curling my toes and forcing my legs to spread wider than I thought possible. "Just a little longer. I'm not ready to let go yet."

He wasn't ready to go, but I was barely hanging on. To my sanity, to reality, to the sensations tightening deep in my core pleading to be released. Cash circled his hips and hit nerves deep inside me I'd never felt before, and each one thrust ground my teeth, deafened my ears, curled my toes, and excommunicated every thought from my head except Cash and the torturous climb he pressed toward our completion.

I said goodbye to the ability to form words, to do anything other than hold on and pray I didn't internally combust. We were snakes, writhing and twisting, anticipating when that final movement would deliver the killing bite.

"You've barely even stirred the floor above us. C'mon, give me something louder than that," he chuckled, nipping my earlobe.

Had I said something? I felt as if I existed in nuclear fallout where the absence of sound deafened my ears. There was simply too much of *everything*, that every sound in the room had distilled into white noise.

"I'm there, Harlow." The rumble of his voice in my ear pulled me from my musings, "You've been such a good girl holding on for me. Let's fall together."

Thank every deity known to man that he'd suggested we let go. Because I'd never thought being praised would be something that would twist me so tight, I'd lose my breath.

"Harlow," my name falling from his lips was both exclamation and exaltation and filled me from the cellular level. That was all it took and the both of us leapt from the mountain of desire into the cooling satisfaction of our completion.

CHAPTER 17

CASH 

Something buzzing pulled me into consciousness. I lifted my head in search of the annoying sound, realizing the pair of us barely made it through cleaning up before we'd collapsed in a heap of limbs that hadn't shifted through the entire night. I saw my cell phone screen light up from inside my pants still laying on the floor exactly where I'd discarded them the night before.

Rather than jump to discover whatever request urgently awaited my reply, I sank back into the warmth of the bed and the quiet comfort of waking up next to such a wonderful woman.

"mmtime is it?" came from beneath one of the pillows.

"About seven thirty," I told her, rolling over so we'd be face to face once her head popped up from beneath the pillows.

I felt oddly serene. The usual string of worries and anxieties that would make themselves known the moment I opened my eyes, for the moment lay silent. My heart beat at a normal pace, my muscles were deliciously lax, and the only thoughts that tickled through my mind were finding ways to spend more time with Harlow.

There were so many things I wanted to know. Little things. Like if she liked scary movies. Did she drink coffee in the morning? What she did for fun? Or hell, what she did for a job? I wanted to order room service and spend the whole day lying in this pillow and blanket fort we'd buried ourselves under and have her unspool the entire history of what made her, her.

"I should go and find my sister," she grumbled. "I'm sure she's worried since I didn't make it back to our room last night."

"I'm sure she realizes you're a grown woman and more than likely figures you spent it with me."

Her skin was satin soft. I couldn't stop touching it. Like my fingers acted on their own accord, needing to feel that softness in order to continue to function.

"I don't know about that. One-night stands aren't usually my thing."

Was this a one-night stand? It didn't feel that way. Though, we both checked out in the morning. The weekend would be over.

"Well, before you go a few more rounds with your sister, you need sustenance. How about breakfast?"

She threw the covers back and nodded.

"You're so beautiful like this," I told her, admiring how the sunlight kissed her hair.

"Thank you." She smiled at me like I was the very sunshine lighting her up.

Even first thing in the morning, she tasted sweeter than a sigh.

"What about me?" I asked, taking her hand and running it over my chest. "Do you think I'm beautiful?"

I'd never sought anyone's approval before. I had no idea why I needed hers. But, feeling her fingertips take an exploratory journey down my chest, tracing over the tattoos on my pecs, dancing across the softness of my chest and belly I'd always wished was as well defined as Beckett, Presley, and Harris, I realized how badly I wanted her to look at me with heat in her eyes, too.

She nodded; her eyes rounded with empathy that I never expected to see. As if she understood what it was like being the oldest and least successful. That she had the ability to peek into the deepest recesses of *my* insecurities and know what demons lived there.

"Addictive." She bit her lip, her fingers tracing even lower. "Intoxicating." She leaned in and fed me her tongue at the exact moment she cradled my sack, running the pad of her thumb over my growing erection.

I guess breakfast could wait.

Group Text from Beckett: Harris & Cash do you want to meet up at ESPN? We can do brunch after the interview?

Harris: Sure thing. But Cash may be…occupied.

Harris: I tried knocking on his door ten minutes ago and there was a lot of moaning going on in there 😳 😏

Harris: Looks like the magic of Vegas bagged a second Murray

Beckett: I leave you alone for one day and you find a girlfriend?

Presley: Aww, leave him alone.

Presley: Harlow is fantastic.

Harris: He's definitely punching above his weight class

Harris: Shit. 😬

Harris: I meant bc she's so much better than you…not because, you know she's umm

Presley: JFC Harris. 😵‍🥴

Presley: Ignore Harris. As per usual

I was too high on life to even be the slightest bit bothered by Harris' foot-in-mouth moment. Harlow was my goddess. Inside and out. *My* goddess? Shit. I held no claim to her.

Cash: On my way

I didn't bother responding to the rest. I'm sure Harris was buried deep with embarrassment and there was no need drawing that out. While Harlow had to rush off to find her sister who sent frantic texts from the moment she woke up, she promised we could have dinner after the tournament and spend our last night together. *Our last night.*

Running through the options for an oozingly romantic location for dinner in my head, I'd been so distracted standing waiting for my Uber that I didn't notice the group of goons to my nine o'clock. That was until one cold clocked me.

"Dino sends his regards." The bald guy in a black leather jacket spit on me as I landed hard on the pavement.

"You seem to have forgotten your little agreement." A taller one gathered my hair in his hand and smashed my face against the concrete. I could taste blood, but didn't know where on my face the injury was."

"Guys," I held tightly to conscious thought, forcing my brain and mouth to work together for a few more minutes. "I'm not breaking any of Dino's rules."

"Heard you have a big game today." The third goon aimed for

a sharp foot to my sack, but thankfully I saw him pull that shiny boot back and rolled at the last second, taking the brunt of the kick in my thigh instead.

"It's not even a series event." I coughed, forcing my brain not to disassemble when I needed it most. "Our contract only ever covered series sponsored events, so tell Dino to eat a dick."

"You win today… you better believe Dino will be shoving yours down your throat while he extricates your winnings out of your bones."

"Hey!" Security rushed to my assistance, directing someone to notify the police.

"He's watching you." The spitter lobbed another one in my direction before hopping into a car, rushing off in a squeal of tires and a gunned engine.

The hotel team helped me into their infirmary, cleaned me up, and asked me some questions to file a report. I answered their questions. I knew the moment the police saw the name Dino Frangioni, somehow the report would mysteriously fall into a shredder.

"What the hell happened to you?" Harris was like a yorkie, jumping at my ankles the moment I walked into the studio.

"Jeez, and I even changed my shirt before coming over."

"Be serious, Cash, you look like hell. I thought you were with Harlow."

"I was. Where are Beckett and Presley?"

Harris pointed at the TV screens above our heads in the waiting room. The tv labeled "Studio 3C" showed Beckett getting mic'd and someone running some powder along Presley's temple. He looked positively nauseous.

"C'mon, Pres...pull it together." I muttered to myself, "This is your life now."

"He's been a wreck all morning." Harris told me, standing next to me in front of the bank of televisions. "Is considering calling Texas and telling them thanks, but no thanks. Says he can't handle the pressure."

That was insane. It was nerves talking. There was no one better suited for a Division 1A coaching job than him. As the brother who sat in the stands watching Beckett, he knew everything there was to know about competitive swimming. I didn't have a single doubt he would bring their swim program to glory similar to Stanford, Michigan, and Florida.

"How long till the interview rolls?" I asked Harris.

I arrived way later than anticipated. Obviously. I tried to clean myself up and look as presentable as possible, but some arnica cream and sunglasses can't hide most of what those assholes did.

"About twenty minutes." He unlocked his iPhone to confirm the time.

"How do I get to the sound studio?" I pointed down the hall and started walking without his directions.

"Fourth door on the right. If the red light is on, you won't be able to get in."

Thankfully, it wasn't.

"Pres." I was in front of him in three long strides.

"What the hell happened to your face?" He practically fell out of his chair. I knew they messed me up good, but that had to be his own nerves. My face didn't look *that* bad. Just a little bruised.

"Long story," I batted his hand away from my cheek, grabbing onto it to force him to focus on me. "Look, you look like you're going to pass out and also throw up. Deep breaths."

"He's fine." Beckett called to me from his chair. "We've been sitting here talking the whole time."

"Have you looked at him?" I asked, turning to look at Beckett from over my shoulder. "If not for the powder and makeup, the poor kid would be green."

"Pres, you are going to kill it as a swimming coach. You are meant for that role."

He opened his mouth to say something, but I held up my hand so I could finish.

"Being Beckett's little brother gave you an opportunity that no one else had. Intimate observations. You saw the life of an Olympian up close. You know where he struggled because you sat at the dinner table every night listening to him talk about it, and then saw him work through those problems the next day at the pool. You are going to be the absolute best swim coach this generation has known. I can feel it in my bones. The Big 12 doesn't know what's coming for them."

"I'm sorry, sir. We're about to start filming."

I pulled him into a rough hug, told Beckett to break a leg, and saw myself out.

"Damn, Cash...you gave me goosebumps." Harris held up his arm as proof.

"Pay attention." I pointed at the TV screen. "That will probably be you someday, too."

CHAPTER 18

Harlow

The last thing I wanted or needed was a confrontation with Lennox. Especially after such a glorious night with Cash. I woke up to a slew of worried text messages.

Me: With Cash. Going for bfast. Will be up soon.

Of course, "going for breakfast" turned into another session of "how long can Cash keep Harlow on a razor's edge of need before she comes." That was new. Having someone else create that kind of out of your head blind need? Damn, I don't know if I'd be okay with not experiencing that anymore once the weekend ended. I refused to even let my brain hone in on those thoughts. I needed to keep my head in the game. I had a tournament to win today, otherwise all of this effort would be for naught.

"Look, I honestly am not trying to hurt you." Lennox said as soon as I opened the door.

And an entire evening of good feelings deflated faster than the world's land-speed record.

"Lennox, I don't want to do this with you."

I threw my bag down on the dresser and peeled off my boots. I definitely could not wear those a second day in a row. In fact, I had no idea what I even had in my wardrobe that worked for day two of a tournament.

"I am who I am. Accept me or don't. But the days of me ignoring and internalizing your passive aggressive comments every time I come within five feet of food? Those days are behind us. You're not my mom. And supporting me doesn't involve counting my calories for me."

Lennox crossed her arms, screwing up her mouth as if something snotty was about to come out of it.

"Len, I'm going to take a shower and then go find something to wear for tonight's tournament. The tournament that I'm playing in to alleviate some of *your* stress because I love you. Either we can continue to bicker, and you can tell me all the reasons as a nurse you worry about me and *encourage* me to lose weight as an act of love, or we can reset, go shopping and enjoy the rest of the weekend."

She chose the latter.

The second round of the tournament felt lightyears more intense than day one. First, there were only four tables instead of the sixteen we'd played the day prior. They split up the top players from each table so no one played with anyone who sat at their table. That meant Cash was at Table Four and I was at Table One, according to the chart.

"How are you feeling, Hollywood?"

Cash wrapped his arm around me, drowning me in that cedar and citrus smell that had practically overnight become a comfort.

"I'm feelin—Jesus Christ! Cash, what the hell happened to your face?"

"I had some amazing sex with a real panther in bed. Clawing, shaking, moaning...who knew edging someone would produce such...obvious results.”

I raised his sunglasses away from his face so I could take a look at the damage. He didn’t protest or try to stay my hand. It was bad. The entire socket in his left eye was puffy and blue purple.

“Be serious.”

He huffed and pulled me against his chest, resting his chin on my head.

“Dino sent some of his friends to say hello this morning. It doesn’t feel as bad as it looks, I promise.”

“You need to go to the police.” I pulled back, looking him dead in his poor puffy and swollen eye.

“I already did.”

“Maybe you shouldn’t play if this is his way of saying hello.”

“Fuck that. He can’t intimidate me. I’m free of him. His stupid goons can use me as a sandbag all they want. I’m not going to let him scare me away from doing what I have every right to do. Legally and as a customer of this resort.”

I didn’t know the whole Dino situation. Just the bits and pieces from dinner the night previous. I’d meant to ask him about it, but we satisfied more pressing needs when we got back to the hotel room.

“Dino isn’t worth the air you waste on his name. Let’s talk about other things. Like how delicious you look in this top. Is it new?”

He ran his nose down my neck, drawing my pulse point to his mouth with a seductive lick. My pulse skittered and as if magnetized, collected right where his lips played and teased. Within seconds I was boneless and had trouble remembering my own name.

“Get a room!”

I heard one of his brothers hooting from somewhere off to our left.

“Fucking assholes.” He huffed a laugh. “They wanted to come watch us play. Be our cheerleaders or some shit.”

"You're at table four," I told him, pointing to where people slowly began gathering.

"I don't care about the game. I want to know if there's anything new under this top that I can look forward to seeing later."

He made a show of trying to pull my top out to peek down my shirt. With a giggle I swatted away his hand, accepting instead a last parting kiss.

"Remember what I told you yesterday, Hollywood. Keep up the tease, mask the tells."

I flipped the hair hanging over my shoulder from my high ponytail and turned on my shoe to sashay toward my table. Loving the sound of Cash's laughter over the din of voices collecting on the poker floor.

"Haha, I love it!" he called.

Only me, Queen of the Awkward, didn't *quite* hear him correctly. I turned toward him, overflowing with joy and called, "I love you, too!"

To which his face melted in confusion. That was going to live rent free in my head for the entirety of the poker tournament. If I had any hope of winning this thing, being reminded of how absolutely awkward I was, definitely would hinder that.

CHAPTER 19

CASH 

I t was all of the noise in the space. Total misunderstanding. No one had feelings for someone else after *two days*. There was no way. But, maybe there was a possibility of an *us*. After this weekend. I didn't even like Atlantic City. There was no reason I needed to live there. It just happened to be where I existed.

Beckett wanted me in San Diego with him. Had suggested giving me a position at Ginger Root, where his now fiancée was CEO. I didn't know anything about the organic beverage industry. I certainly didn't want to be the albatross around Lane's neck. Something she had to tolerate out of a sense of devotion to my brother. But it did mean that I had options I could consider.

Despite being the championship round, I played with puppies. Their tells were so obvious I honestly felt as if I was being punked. Thirty minutes in and the first guy at my table was already out. An hour in, and two and three were gone, and my last opponent and I were already in heads up.

We both had decent cards. I had the beginnings of straight with suited eight nine diamonds with a ten of diamonds and king of diamonds on the table. He had a ten and a king, anticipating a full house. I had the higher probability of winning and nailed the guy's coffin when a queen of diamonds dropped. Nearly a straight but having five suited cards gave me a flush and the win. My brothers stood in the little seating section they'd assembled for day two, hooting and hollering my success.

I sat off to the side observing the other games in play. Table three still had four people playing, two was in heads up as well, and Harlow and some greasy looking guy who stepped out of the seventies were in a battle of matching pots and never-ending calls. He covered his tells well. In four hands I still hadn't figured out what they were. Of course, I wasn't close enough to see what cards they played or how he handled his bets. But from where I sat his face was a mask of stone. For the first time since we'd taken off on this little adventure I wondered if he would take Harlow down.

"What's her all in?" he asked the dealer.

"Twenty-four," the dealer replied.

The little hustler had quite the stack. It was all just chips, not actual money. But collecting twenty-four hundred dollars from a five-person table? Impressive. He backed away from his all in, choosing to call instead. The tables must have turned, and he had the lesser amount of chips.

Off at table two there were cheers as a woman in a jean jacket and cowboy boots took the win. She got less than seconds of my focus. I felt like I needed to watch every movement of Harlow's game, in some weird psychic connection offering her my support. It was bullshit of course. I knew me watching had nothing to do with her winning or not. But it alleviated the helplessness of fate deciding.

He took the pot, but it was peanuts compared to her all in. She was still easily up by two thousand. Personally, I'd never call an all-in unless I knew I had very little chance of losing, and I'd never back off from an all-in inquiry once I made it. I saw the smallest glimmer in Harlow's eyes when the next round of cards was dealt.

There was blood in the water now. He'd opened his own

artery and teased all of the sharks into the dark waters. She knew how much was in his pot. She knew exactly how much money it would take to force him to go all in. And if she got lucky enough to get a solid hand—his game was over.

"Fourteen," she told the dealer, stacking her chips in the pot, forcing a heads up.

The pair stood while the dealer doled out the rest of the cards. She had pocket jacks. A solid bet on her part. Not really risky as the likelihood of taking the round was pretty high. He had a queen, king, suited. Decent, but since she held his jack of clubs in her hand, she removed the opportunity for a flush. He could still beat her with a straight. But since she had a pair of jacks, she held the higher probability of getting a full house or a three of a kind. The final card turned, a six of diamonds, which was no help to either of them, and Harlow took the round with her pocket jacks.

"You fat bitch," the guy sneered. "What business do you even have being *in* this tournament? Are you cheating? Is someone coaching you? You told the dealer Friday you barely knew how to play, yet you're going to the final round? Challenge!" he screamed pointing at her. "I call challenge."

Harlow looked at me, stunned. I was already up and closing in on that piece of shit. Security was hot on my tail. They must have seen the rage on my face, and the set of bruises that said I wasn't afraid to get dirty.

"Check her ear. She's gotta be wearing a piece. There's no way she could make it this far!" he continued to shout.

Security took hold of his arm, trying to calmly and without incident escort him away from the playing tables.

"She won fair." I told the officials starting to gather. "I watched from over there."

I pointed to the chair that was now tipped over from me exiting it so quickly.

"If she'd been wearing a piece or any number of things, I would have seen it."

Someone from the hotel escorted Harlow over to the hallway by the bathrooms.

"Green card," I requested.

They handed me one so that I could exit and return before the next round started. It only worked when your game had completed, and others were still in play.

"One for her, too." I nodded toward Harlow who looked shaken while she stood hugging herself.

"Follow me."

She fell into step next to me. Her upset rolled off her in waves. If she had any hope of succeeding in the next round, she needed to find that glowy confidence she'd exuded through the whole first round.

"In here." I pointed to a private bathroom.

"Cash... we can't go in here. This is an accessible bathroom. What if it's the only one on this floor?"

"There's two more right next door."

The door shut with a soft snick. Her breath hitched, but her eyes were still acres of meandering forests clouded by rain.

"You are beautiful."

I ran my hand down her cheek, cupping her neck and shoulder. Her pulse jackrabbited beneath my palm, beating in wild and erratic patterns.

"Say it, Hollywood. Repeat it."

"Cash, this is silly. It's not like it's the first time someone has insulted me."

"It's the first time someone has insulted something that *I* find to be deliriously sexy, and I don't take kindly to people dishonoring something I cherish. Now say it."

"Cash...we need to get back to the tournament."

"There's still three people at table three trying to figure out the difference between the hole in the ground and their asshole. They're easily twenty minutes if not thirty away from determining a winner. Now, I've asked nicely, Harlow. I want to hear you tell me. If I don't hear it in the next five seconds, I'm upping the ante."

CHAPTER 20

Harlow

This was insane. If I huddled in a bathroom and cried every time someone slung a fatphobic insult at me, I'd never leave the bathroom. That Cash got so insulted in my honor was cute and all, but wholly unnecessary.

"Harlow...my last request. Tell me."

I wasn't going to. I didn't need any of his reaffirming, cognitive behavior psychology, pattern rewriting. No matter how hot this protective, *no one insults what I cherish*, streak was.

I was wrapped in his arms faster than my brain could process I'd been bound against his chest and locked by his arms.

"I don't want that needle dicked little fucker to even get a centimeter of space in that pretty head of yours when your whole focus needs to be on getting through the next round."

His mouth was so close to my ear, the word shiver didn't even fully describe what my body did in response. It was a whole-body jolt, followed by bone softening pleasure seeping through my bloodstream.

That delicious sensation distracted me from Cash's plundering fingers, which somehow insinuated themselves beneath my dress, and under the lace panties I'd purchased just before the tournament with Cash in mind.

"Is this new?"

He asked, running his fingers along the seam of it, staring at me staring at him in the bathroom mirror. All I could do was nod. I couldn't stop gaping at his reflection, unable to take my focus away from the image of his hand working me beneath my dress.

"What color is it?" Hhe asked, choosing to have me describe it instead of just lifting up the skirt of my dress and looking his fill.

"The same color as the dress," I told him.

"Green. For good luck. But you don't need luck, Hollywood. You know why?"

As he continued to whisper words in my ear, his finger insinuated itself beneath the elastic of my panties and pressed against my already throbbing clit.

"Tell me, Hollywood. Why don't you need luck."

"Because I have you." I gasped, barely able to form words.

"You do. You'll always have me," he said, "But that's not why. You don't need luck because you are invincible. Wonder Woman. Beauty and brains, that mind of yours sees each of your opponent's weaknesses and capitalizes on them. You're a warrior. A stunning, sexy, delicious warrior."

He kissed my temple, pressing against my clit with purpose. His thick cock nudged against my ass, pushing me against the fingers that tickled and enticed toe-curling bliss to rocket through my whole body.

"And if you do as you're told...I'll sling you so high into the solar system, the only thoughts left in your mind will be how worshipped you are by the man standing behind you. So, tell me, Hollywood. I want to hear you say it."

His finger circled my clit, softening in pressure. I bit my lips to prevent myself from begging for what my body screamed for. He pressed me against the counter, held me firm with nowhere to go. I couldn't cant my hips to force his finger against my clit or roll to my tiptoes. He'd checkmated me. Without doing exactly as he requested, I'd be stuck dangling in the in-between.

"Tell me." He demanded, his eyes full of fire.

"I'm beautiful."

I whispered, a tear rolling down my cheek. The moment that little drop of water broke free and slid down, Cash collected it with his free hand, kissing away the remnant damp.

"You are, Harlow. A gorgeous, unflappable warrior. And what are you going to do when we get back out there?"

His finger danced over my sensitive nub, causing my pulse to surge and my ears to deafen.

"Win," I moaned into my orgasm. "I'm gonna win."

If not for being pressed against Cash's chest and hips, I would have collapsed to the floor. I felt as if my entire body had imploded and couldn't summon up the energy to reassemble.

"So good." Cash stared at my reflection, bringing his fingers to his lips and sucking. "Best thing I've had all day."

Once I had full function back in my limbs, Cash helped me straighten up, and made sure I could stand on my own before letting go.

"I want to see." He lifted up the skirt of my dress. "I lack enough imagination to picture my present."

My dress was a loose pleated cotton with some stretch. I lifted it high enough to expose the green lace balconette bra lifting and cradling the girls and the lace cheeky panties.

"I approve, Hollywood."

He cradled my face and kissed me one last time. "We need to get back. Remember, you are Wonder Woman. And don't forget to mask your tells!"

With that he yanked open the door and walked back into the crowd. How the fuck was I supposed to focus on anything other than the flutter in my lady parts and Cash's name beating in time with my pulse?

Being at the final table of a casino poker tournament is much more intimidating than I thought it would be. Especially when there were only four people. Me, Cash, another woman in a jean jacket and cowboy boots, and some old guy who looked like he'd expired right in the middle of the game if it got too stressful.

The other woman had the most obvious tell. I spotted it between the fourth and fifth hand. She chewed on a toothpick and smiled with it tucked between her lips when she had a bad hand, and twirled that nasty little piece of wood in her mouth when she had a good hand. I wanted to bump her out just so I didn't have to tamp down the vomit crawling up my throat.

She clearly felt something toward me, as she continually asked the dealer what my pot was. Not Cash's pot, or the old guys, just mine. I had no idea how much everyone had in their pots. They all looked relatively even to me.

Cash drew first blood, however, going heads up with the old man and taking him out with a full house. And then there were three. Annie Oakley kept her laser focus on me, challenging me hand after hand, trying to draw me from overcommitting my pot. I refused to take her bait, and eventually it was glaringly evident that her pot had bled out to its final breath. I looked at Cash, trying to discern his thoughts beneath those glasses, but he was stone faced.

"What's her pot?" I asked the dealer.

"Two-fifty," the dealer replied.

I threw two hundred and fifty chips into the pot, Cash folded, and we went to heads up. I had a pair of sevens, not the best hand in the world but nearly all the face cards had already been played, so the likelihood of her having more than a single face card was small.

Damn, Cash would be so proud. I made a mental note to tell him about how well I'd been paying attention to the card play. Annie Oakley turned over her cards and she had a three, ten suited hearts, obviously hoping for a straight. When the flop dropped, the dealer gave us a pair of twos, one heart, one club, keeping her straight draw alive but also giving me hope for a full house. I saw Cash shake his head just the teeniest bit. His brain must have been calculating the probability. The turn gave her another heart, a six. The final card wasn't a help for either of us, a nine of clubs, but I held the pair, and Annie Oakley was out of the game.

"Ten minutes!"

One of the Aria staff called, and I snuck into the hallway where the bathrooms were. I expected to see Cash hot on my heels, but he didn't come. I paced, waited some more, and peeked out onto the tournament floor to see if I could place him. He was nowhere to be seen. What the hell?

CHAPTER 21

CASH 

Whether Harlow wanted to admit it or not, she took to poker like a fish in water. I watched in awe as she deflected challenges from the other two at the table. Like a graceful swan, lazily swimming figure eights around the other two, I had no idea if it truly came easy to her or if she calculated statistics and probabilities in her head.

And that old lady who looked like she was on her way to the rodeo? I expected that pot check after pot check would knock Harlow off her game. Throw her. Cause her to back down and lose her focus. Yet, she calmly raised her eyebrow in challenge each time the old lady circled looking for a weak point.

When they went head to head I nearly hooted with delight. My celebration was short-lived, as I caught Dino out of the corner of my eye pushing his way into the stands with his collection of goons. I wouldn't give them the satisfaction. My sunglasses covered most of the damage they'd done to my face anyway. Besides, I had the scent of Harlow's orgasm still teasing my nose and that set my spine in steel.

I hadn't lied when I told his minions that Dino had no control and no reach. The lawyers had said vetted tournaments, invitation games, and high stakes competitions with national ranking. This was none of those things. It was a flash in the pan contest intended to drum up interest over the long weekend.

"You can see yourself out," I told Dino, shoulder checking him into the wall.

"I guess my guys didn't deliver my message. I would hate for you to lose the only part of you that seems to be successful."

He nodded toward the chair Harlow just exited, and I saw red. Not because I gave a shit what he thought about me, but because he'd somehow planted enough of his shitty men that he'd somehow figured out about Harlow and me as a *couple*.

"You win this game, turn over your pot to me, and we'll walk away from this. As an added bonus I'll let you keep that sorry little sissy dick that you can't keep in your pants whenever Brunhilda over there jiggles."

I wanted to punch him. Crack him right in that shit eating maw of his and force him to swallow his teeth. Instead, I'd played him at his own game.

"I would love to signal my brothers right now, and have them exact the same amount of revenge your banded group of baboons did earlier this morning. But I have a game to get back to, and I'm not interested in spending any extra energy on a piece of shit like you than I already have. You want my pot. Fine. You can have whatever I win. But this is the end, Dino. After this you leave me the fuck alone."

He looked at me long and hard before extending his hand.

"Don't try to fool me. There's no way you won't win this. Don't fall on a fucking sword just because you want between her thighs later. I catch you throwing the game, and you'll be choking on your own dick as promised. You as the champion."

"Me as the champion, and you leave me alone?" I asked.

He nodded, shoving his hand even further toward me. That he thought I believed his handshake was worth anything was a damn joke. The only thing that kept him in control were laws that could land him in jail, not some gentleman's pact.

"I'll beat her. By the end of this round, I'll be the Champion."

I told him, turning and walking toward the gaming tables again. "I've made an intensive study of every one of her tells."

I stalked toward the table, laser focused on the task at hand.

"I wondered where you'd meandered off to." She took my hand, smiling up at me.

"Just having a chat with those assholes." I cocked my head toward my brother who waved and hooted wildly when they saw us looking at them.

"Remember what I told you. Keep those tells close to the chest. Even with me. Don't give me any chance to swoop in and find your weakness. You're a warrior."

I wanted to kiss her. To hold her jaw and plunder her mouth, but I couldn't draw any attention to us. Her eyes shone with excitement, she glowed with pride, and I wanted to remember her just as she looked at that very moment.

"Don't pull any punches, Hollywood. If you find a way to go for the jugular, you do it."

I didn't give her a chance to respond.

"This is the final round." The pit boss stood between Harlow and me, creating far too much drama for this tournament. "Do you both agree to the terms of the payouts of this round, all or nothing, as predetermined by the players and authorized by the Aria Resort and Casino?"

I nodded. Looking at Harlow out of the corner of my eye, she nodded as well.

"Best of luck. Dealer up."

Everyone started to clap and hoot. I tried not to roll my eyes at the pomp and circumstance, but when I turned to Harlow and saw the flush in her cheeks and the stars in her eyes, I remembered when these kinds of things used to be a rush like that.

We were each given an even distribution of chips, five hundred dollars each. There were two strategies, hit your opponent with high pots out of the gate to draw down their coiffeurs and hope for the best, or draw it out for a long game to mentally exhaust them.

Since Harlow no doubt possessed mental acuity in spades, I'd have been smarter to take the former, but given she was inexperienced, any aggressive bid strategies would have her folding to protect her pot rather than dumping it in and betting on a bluff. Opening bids in the championship round were fifty dollars for the small blind and a hundred for the big. Instead, if I raised the bids slowly, like a frog in a boiling pot, I'd have a better chance of reeling her in.

Right out of the gate, the fates gifted me with pocket kings. I sat and waited to bet, watching her like a predator. I made a case study of every shift, toss of her hair, and tug of her lip. I had no idea which was an actual tell and which was theatrics, but in my head all I could think over and over again was *good girl*. She masked those tells beautifully.

"Fifty." She raised after the flop which meant the three cards the dealer placed must be something she needed: a ten of clubs, a queen of hearts, and a two of diamonds. Potential queen pair, possible ten pair, all of those things I could beat with my pair of kings.

"Call." I matched her.

The dealer revealed the turn card, a jack of diamonds. No help for me, but I put in another fifty to see what she'd do. If she thought I had a pair of jacks, and I was right in assuming she had a pair of queens, she wouldn't be able to resist matching me.

"Call," she replied, the sweetest lilt in her voice.

The river was a three of spades. I checked, and she followed suit. The dealer asked for our cards, and my pair of kings took out her pair of queens, and I was awarded a look of unabashed surprise that she didn't have time to think about masking.

We played a few rounds of cat and mouse, neither of us having any truly spectacular hands and we traded best top card pot draws. By my estimation I was still ahead of her by roughly two hundred dollars. Nearly halfway there. The waitress brought us bottles of water while the dealer changed out decks, and the next round was dealt. Jack, ten, suited diamonds. Not the best hand but workable. I doubled the pot. Harlow stared at me long and hard. Her face was a stoic mask but I could tell she was desperate to read any kind of tell from my face.

"Call." She matched my bet.

I think she thought I was bluffing. Possibly. I bluffed her out of a hundred dollars a few rounds back.

The flop gave me a king in diamonds, but I held back from betting, and sat in wait to see what she'd do.

"Raise," she called, throwing another fifty dollars into the pot.

Quite the predicament. She could easily be bluffing me as I had her. Trying to draw me out, get me to throw all the money she'd lost to me back into the pot so that she could ensnare me. There were few possibilities she had that could give her that kind of confidence. The most likely was a flush—a run of face cards. I threw fifty in, willing to see where she led me. The river and the turn gave me the diamonds that I sought though she checked me waiting to see what I would do.

I could only assume she had nothing if she left the pot as low as she did.

"Raise." I tossed in another fifty, curious if she'd take the bait this late in the hand. If she folded, she'd lose what she already had in there. But if she called and put another fifty in the pot she risked depleting her already dwindling pile.

"See." She placed fifty into the middle, trying to bore through my sunglasses to get a long look at my eyes. "Raise."

Another fifty went in. It took every ounce of willpower not to raise my eyebrows in her direction. I hoped she knew what she was doing.

I tossed my fifty in to make it even and the dealer asked us both to reveal our cards.

We'd both been mining for diamonds. The only difference was hers were beautifully in order six through ten. And just like that, the little grasshopper bested the ant.

"Well done."

I couldn't hold back my praise. That was a ninja level move, and she deserved to be recognized. She winked at me but said nothing.

It seemed like hours we traded pots back and forth between the two of us. She honestly surprised me with how well she did. They raised the opening bids (called blinds) to one hundred and two hundred, and given the slow progression I decided it was time to dial the difficulty level up a notch.

I didn't even receive a matched pair, but I had an ace of clubs, so at least I had the upper hand of the highest card in the deck. She checked, I checked. The next three cards didn't give me much. But there were two clubs in the group of three so I could at least use that. I threw in the new minimum bid which was one hundred. Harlow followed suit, watching my face the whole time the dealer dropped the next card. Damn, she was getting good at anticipating when someone's guard would be down. Someone's but not mine.

The next card to drop was a king, also in a club. I held hope for a straight. But even if I didn't it was a card that would signal any person with less experience to start hitting the gas on their bets. I threw in another minimum bid, she matched, watching me again as the final chip came down. A queen of spades, but there was enough on the table to potentially spook her into thinking I had a straight.

"Raise," I said, throwing in two hundred dollars into the pot.

Her hand lingered over her chips. She regarded me for eternity, fingering her stack before finally throwing her cards in and folding. Smart, but also glaringly transparent of a rookie.

She was down to her last three hundred dollars, and the dealer gave me a pair of nines. I saw the truth in her eyes. The fear that this was the end of the line for her. She valiantly tried to hide it, biting her lip hard as she tossed her required hundred dollars into the pot.

I took two hundred dollars in chips and called her all in, putting us in heads up. I couldn't bait her. Force her into false hope. The least I could do was drive the knife in while looking at her in the face. Make it a quick execution.

The dealer turned our cards over and my pair beat her six with a king kicker. She knew it. I watched her lip quiver as the flop produced nothing that could help either one of us: a ten, a four, and a jack. And a juicy tear rolled down her cheek as the turn produced a second four, giving me two pairs, essentially nailing her coffin shut. The river gave her a second six, but at that point it was too late. I'd already won.

I stood, going to her, pulling her into a hug. The cheers around me fell on deaf ears. The only thing I heard was Harlow sobbing into my chest, telling me how badly she wanted to do right by her sister, and she failed.

CHAPTER 22

Harlow

Logical me always knew I stood little chance against Cash. But the emotional side, the side that unabashedly followed Cash down a rabbit hole of whatever our little dalliance was these past two days—she had been nursing a kernel of hope that Cash would find a way to gallantly fall on a sword and let me take the win.

I shouldn't have started crying. That was totally unsportsmanlike. Was poker a sport? Do sportsmanlike behaviors even apply to a game of bluffing and lying? Regardless, sobbing like a baby without its bottle was not the high point of my Vegas vacation, that's for sure.

"Get away from her you piece of shit! You...I don't even have a word for you. How dare you. How *dare* you pretend you comfort her when you were just chatting it up with that asshole over there telling him about how you convinced the chubby girl to fall for you so you could learn her tells and beat her!"

Lennox's fingernails dug so deep and hard into the flesh of my arm that I thought for sure she drew blood. Her eyes bugged practically out of her head, her voice screeching like a mother bear protecting its cub. Not that I knew what a bear would sound like, but the way Lennox's voice separated and screeched, I assumed it had to be something quite close.

"Lennox, what the hell are you talking about?" I asked, looking to Cash for clarification.

"Don't even bother to open your mouth, you greasy, slimeball, scheister."

"Cash?" Harris and Presley approached, their smiles plummeting straight off their faces as they watched my sister go thermonuclear.

"Cash, what the fuck is she talking about?" Presley asked.

"Cash would never do anything to Harlow. I don't think I've ever seen him so taken by someone." Harris tried to soothe Lennox from whatever tree she climbed up in her head, imagining I needed protection. "I'm Harris, by the way. You must be Harlow's sister."

"Stay away from us," Lennox continued. "Like she isn't hurt enough being taken for everything she had by some fixed fucking game between your brother and that asshole in the leather jacket. I heard them talking, so don't even try to deny it."

"Cash?" I tilted his sunglasses onto his head and all I saw was gaping pits of despair. The irises of his eyes were so wide and so blue, if I got too close, I felt like I could fall in and drown in them. "Is it true?"

"Congrats, Murray."

Said asshole in the jacket came sauntering up, clapping Cash on the shoulder. If I hadn't been making a study of that face for the last god knows how many hours, I wouldn't have seen him grind his molars and try to mask a flare of disgust that disappeared as fast as it appeared.

"Just let me know where I can collect my pot."

"You're back with Dino?!" Presley practically screamed, his face turning a shade of puce I didn't think capable on human flesh. "I thought you said he was the one who fucked up your face? Why are you splitting pots with Dino, Cash?"

"Dino needs proper motivation in order to follow court

orders, isn't that right, Dino?" Cash *growled*. I'd never heard a sound that full of rage before in my entire life. It was so feral, so laced with acid, it made the hairs on my arms stand up.

"Either I tow the line or I, what was it you said again? I'd be eating my sorry little dick? Well, you can choke on it, Dino. My winnings are at the cage. I told them you'd be the one collecting, as usual."

He pushed through the gang of people that surrounded him, shoved his hands in his pockets, and disappeared, head down, into the crowd.

I don't know what made me feel worse. Losing a tournament, I thought I had a chance of winning, or finding out the fix was in and I had no chance of winning it all. Did he truly, actively string me along, convincing me I had a chance of winning? Or was I just that stupid and gullible I believed all of the flowery bullshit he fed me? He didn't just feed it to me. He tied a bib around my neck and served me a buffet of kindness and sweet words.

What an idiot I was.

"...look for easy marks..."

Lennox still ranted as we made our way out of the Casino and upstairs to our room.

"...too sweet and too kind...not experienced enough with men to know when they're stringing you along...should have been a better big sister...asked my friends to take you on dates...maybe then you'd have been less awkward, less trusting."

Her words shattered the last of my resolve. I wasn't some Quasimodo that her stupid juicehead friends needed to take pity on. I was beautiful. A warrior. Capable of incredible things. Like diving face first into something completely foreign, like a poker tournament, and making it to the final round. Regardless of the outcome. No matter that someone like Cash gave me an extra push here and there, I did the work. I followed the cues of everyone at my tables. Me.

I wouldn't let Lennox...or even Cash...take that away from me.

Inside my heart, I wrapped that pride up in the tightest bubble wrap, tucked it gently into a box, and stored it deep down so no one could try to reduce what I did or try to dim that glow.

"Lo?"

I was in the shower. More like I drown myself in hot water and thirty minutes worth of the casino's water supplies, trying to wash away every thought that didn't contribute to my sense of joy or accomplishment.

"In the shower!" I called, washing the ten pounds of makeup off my face, trying to restore some feeling or normalcy.

"Some dude from reception said we hadn't yet checked in with the message he left on our phone. I guess someone dropped a present off at the front desk for you while we were out shopping this afternoon."

Lennox poked her head into the bathroom.

"So, you know, shake a leg! Because one, you're taking all the hot water, and two I want to know what this mystery present is."

Given the bag bore a signature logo that made the mysterious present hard to disguise, what Lennox really wanted to know was who on earth would send *me* something from Louis Vuitton.

No matter what happens today,
you deserve to have this as a souvenir of your
amazing kindness and accomplishment.

With love, Cash Cole Murray.

"I'd send that right back!" She pointed at the card as if the devil itself appeared in our room. "He does not get to do that. He does not get to run off with your winnings and send you an apology bag as a consolation prize."

I hadn't even pulled the bag out yet but I knew what it would look like. It would be the one I stared at for an hour at Caesars. The bandana print, with the soft, glittery logos, and the baby pink interior. A sob balled in my chest, cutting off my air circulation.

"Why would he do this, Len? You said the guy at the door said it arrived while we were shopping. Why would he give me the most perfect gift hours before he would bend me over and hamstring me. It doesn't make any sense."

"You know where he's staying, go down there and confront him. You want me to come with you? I'll tell him what's what".

Instead, I took the chickenshit way out.

> Me: Why? Why would you do this?

> Me: You trick me into believing you were attracted to me just to watch me gloriously nose dive into total shame? What kind of game is that?

> Me: Help me understand this. Because from where I'm standing right now, you spotted an easy mark, and not only forced me to believe things about myself I never would have---but you robbed me of the chance to help my sister.

I stared for ages at my string of texts. Nothing came in response.

CHAPTER 23

CASH 

The text messages hurt. They burned. Like I'd swallowed battery acid and waited patiently for it to corrode my insides and drown me in my own blood.

Not even my brothers wanted anything to do with me. I couldn't process my feelings around that. I'd spent too many years making excuses, cutting out on family obligations, trying to hide away in my shame because I wasn't strong enough to face them in all their wholesome goodness and tell them that Las Vegas had sucked out all the good parts of me, and all that was left was a card hound. Someone who chased the next pot, the next high. A stone that gathered no moss, stayed aloof, unattached, because emotions were kryptonite to a poker champion.

But what it made me was an island. Left to suffer alone when what I craved, yearned for, was someone to put their arm around me, tell me it was okay, and that we'd figure it out together.

> Me: Don't ever doubt you are everything. Gorgeous. Fierce. A Warrior.

I shouldn't have reached out. Should have waited until the morning. Let the shock of what happened wear off. Fucking

Dino. Of course, a stupid decision I'd gone into blindly in my twenties still haunted me more than the years later. I just wanted to be normal. To live a life on main street, with my average car, and my Dockers I bought at Kohl's, having get-togethers on weekends where I grilled ribs or brats and watched Sunday football with my neighbors.

I didn't want this anymore. This fake, glittering half-life. Harlow was so normal, so down to earth, she'd given me a peek into what vacations with my brothers could look like. What it could be like meeting up for dinner or taking long weekends together as a family.

Me: Please trust me.

There was nothing left for me in Vegas. And there was no point staying the night. I'm sure Dino had his men out looking for me anyway. Vegas caused me nothing but problems, fractured relationships, and heartbreak. I never intended on coming back.

CHAPTER 24

Harlow

woke up to two text messages from him. Trust him? Please. He could eat a dick. Trust. I'd given him my trust, and he held it in his hand and looked me dead in the eye when he crumpled it.

"Lo...again with the desk people sent to deliver messages. Jesus. It's not even seven o'clock."

She shuffled back to her bed and flopped into it, yanking the covers back over her head.

"Ms. Prince." The hotel manager addressed me when I opened the door. "Please accept our congratulations on a job well done. We do hope the next time you are in Las Vegas; you will consider booking your stay at the Aria Hotel and Casino once again."

He handed me an envelope, turned on his shiny shoe, and took off in the direction of the elevators. Inside the envelope was a cashier's check for ten thousand dollars. Ten. Thousand. Dollars. And some tax form instructing me to keep it for my records at the end of the year.

"Holy shit. Lennox. Look. Holy shit."

I passed the check over to her, unable to say anything more.

"Why?" she asked. "Was there a mistake? Do they feel sorry

for you because you got tricked into believing that guy was into you? Maybe he's like a serial two timer and the casino is buying your silence so you don't sue."

Fucking Lennox.

"We need to pack. Our flight leaves at ten thirty."

Harris found us in the hallway as we wheeled our luggage toward the elevator.

"Fancy meeting you here." He winked at me and hit the down button. "I guess we're all checking out today."

"Where's your sheister brother?" Lennox did little to hide her ire.

"Checked out last night." He shrugged, rocking back and forth in his gym shoes as we waited for the elevator to arrive.

My dumb heart was having a hard time staying mad. Not that it was for sale just from a gorgeous Louis Vuitton bag, but a few things didn't add up. Like why suddenly I had a cashier's check in my wallet for ten thousand dollars.

"I want to stop at the gaming office," I told Lennox, calling over my shoulder. "Take my bag and wait for me at check out."

"I'll help you with those." Presley magically appeared at the elevators, two drinks in his hand and a backpack strapped to his back. He handed one off to Harris to free his hand to take the rolling suitcase, and led Lennox to reception. Harris continued to follow me, like a lost puppy dog.

"Your brother went to reception. Shouldn't you be checking out with him?"

"Nah. He can handle it. I figured I'd tag along with you, if you don't mind."

"Did Cash give a reason why he left in the middle of the night?"

I couldn't fight the question straining my lips. It seemed strange to leave under the cover of darkness, especially when his brothers were still at the hotel.

"I don't think you've met Beckett yet, have you? Beckett, this is Harlow."

He stood at the gaming office, as if holding a place for me in line. The second I stepped up to the window he stepped out of my way.

"The infamous Harlow. It is so nice to meet you. Congratulations, by the way. I heard you played one hell of a game the last two days."

Beckett was even more panty melting in person than he looked on television. Tall, amber colored eyes, the same stoic look on his face that Cash wore like a second skin until he was engaged in conversation.

"How can I help you, Ms. Prince?" The attendant held out her hand and took the envelope I passed over.

"I'm wondering if you can tell me why I'm receiving this."

"From the poker tournament, of course," she laughed. "This was your winnings."

"But I lost," I told her, confused. "This is Cash's money. He won."

The woman, whose name tag announced her as Betty, pulled out a binder and ran her finger down what looked like the previous night's logs.

"It looks like in the final round, you and Mr. Murray agreed to a winner take all competition with the second-place finisher receiving the winnings, and the first-place finisher receiving bragging rights and the Baccarat trophy."

"That doesn't make sense. Why would the second-place finisher get the money?"

"Who knows dear!" She laughed, patting my hand. "These poker players have all kinds of reasons. Maybe they're about to max out their annual take for the year, and so they just want the points to earn themselves into the next tournament. Sometimes they do it just for bragging rights. There's any number of reasons, but it's nothing unusual for these kinds of things. Kind of cool though, huh? At least you get to go home with something that showed you made it to the finals and almost won the whole thing."

"Thank you, Betty." Beckett shook her hand. "At what level of prize do you provide armed security or a secure transport to the airport?"

"Not for ten thousand dollars, I'm afraid. We had some couple walk out of here yesterday with over a million dollars. They got the armed transport."

"How about a ride to the airport from somewhere other than the front door?"

"I can arrange to have you picked up in the catering bay?"

"That works perfectly." Beckett smiled at her, beaming her a charming smile that nearly singed my own panties, and he wasn't even my type.

Presley and Lennox approached from the left, and Betty signaled to one of the security guards who pushed through a hidden panel in the wall and into a service hallway. We drove to the airport in a smoked out SUV, taking back and side roads instead of the ones along the strip.

Instead of dropping us off at the United Terminal, the car drove around the back of the airport and parked in front of a tiny glass building with a tram idling at the ready.

"This seems a bit excessive for a ten-thousand-dollar check," I said.

"Oh, this isn't the hotel," Harris chuckled. "They gave us the ride and the presidential treatment finding us a way out of the hotel, but that was mostly the Beckett Murray special, as is this."

"This is where we leave you ladies. There is a private ticketing agent right through those doors. The tram will take you directly to the plane after the pilot does his pre-flight checks and just before they open to pre-board."

Beckett extended his hand. I went to shake it and he turned it, palm down, and placed a kiss on my hand.

"When he calls," he whispered, "You might want to answer the phone."

"Iced toffee latte." Harris handed me the cup in his hand.

"And a medium iced matcha tea with coconut milk." He handed the other cup to my sister.

How the hell they knew our coffee orders was beyond me.

"Safe flight, ladies!" He held the door open for us, and helped us step down from the oversized SUV.

"I hope we see you real soon, Harlow." Presley called as we turned toward the private terminal. "I hope we see a whole lot of you."

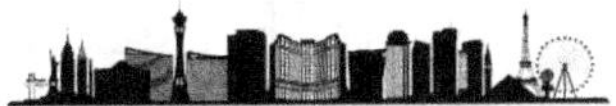

"What the hell was all of *that*?" Lennox asked while we sat in our *upgraded to first class* seats, awaiting takeoff.

"I honestly don't know. I feel like Alice in Wonderland falling down that damn well. Only I keep falling and I have no idea which end is up."

"Are you going to take him back because he flashed some of his seedy poker playing money at you? A Louis Vuitton Bag, some first-class seats, and some prize money is all it takes to buy your forgiveness?"

I'm sure she didn't mean to sound as embittered as she did. It couldn't be easy watching the beginning of someone else's relationship when hers had just recently ended. I'm sure she was still heartbroken.

"I don't even know. So many things feel off. Like they don't add up but not in a bad way. Take the purse, for example. It arrived at one yesterday. One! He bought it just because. Because the second time we met, I was drooling over it, and really torn as to whether or not I wanted to blow all of my winnings on a *bag*. It had nothing to do with what happened last night. Something happened between the first round and the second. Because after the first round..." My body flushed with remembrances. "Let's just say that there is no way he could have been thinking about two-timing me with all the things he said and did."

"Did?" Lennox asked, the question hanging thick in the air between us.

"I'm not going to kiss and tell, but I don't believe there was a single thread of ill intent. It just isn't possible. Not when combined with everything else."

"What everything else?" she asked, smiling her thanks at the flight attendant who passed her a glass of champagne.

"This? His brothers keeping dutiful watch over us, ensuring we safely made it to the airport? The check! The casino said I agreed to the terms yesterday before the game started. The terms stated that the person who won *second place* won the money, and the first-place winner won the trophy. It just doesn't make sense."

"Beckett said he was going to call. I guess you'll just have to wait for the call."

We sat in silence as the captain turned on the seatbelt sign and the airplane taxied to the runway.

"Speaking of." Lennox pulled me out of my musings, just as the plane swung onto the runway and gunned its engines. "...was that Beckett Murray? You know...*the* Beckett Murray? The Olympian?"

CHAPTER 25

Harlow

"Thank you for coming down to the studio." Raven, from the *Bear and Raven Show, escorted* me in heels so high it had to be impossible to walk the streets of Chicago in them into their studio. "It's so much more fun talking to people in person, rather than over the phone."

She pushed through the door and pulled out a swivel chair for me to sit in, in front of a very large microphone.

"Here, put these on. It's going to sound funny for a second until Bear pots us up, but you'll only be able to hear us through these once he starts recording. I don't know how much you know about satellite radio, but we're kind of a hybrid. We're live during the important things like drive times and such, but we also have a lot of pre-recorded content. It means we don't have to be up at three in the morning anymore, which is the best thing about a national syndicated contract."

I could only smile and nod. Raven was next level beautiful. Her hair was a soft rose gold, and it flowed all the way down her back, touching the top of the waist of her jeans. And I'd never been in an air studio before so I was just trying to focus on not throwing up.

"This is Bear. He might look intimidating, but I promise, he's a soft little teddy bear, especially since having twins. The guy may as well tattoo Stay Puft on his ass and call himself a marshmallow."

"Thanks for that rousing introduction, Raven. I'll be sure to have Marley seek you out when it's time to write my obituary. Harlow, nice to meet you in person. I can't wait to hear about your adventures in Las Vegas."

My heart constricted. It had been three long weeks. And I hadn't heard a word from Cash. I'd texted him my thanks for the purse, and the winnings, and even updated him about Lennox and her crazy neighbor. Still his chat on my phone showed delivered but unread.

"I hope coming downtown wasn't a huge hassle," Bear continued, as he slipped his own headphones on and made adjustments as I continued to talk.

"Not at all. I actually work two blocks down, at the opera."

"The opera?" Bear raised his eyebrows, turning to Raven. "Isn't Sera an opera singer?"

"Sera is my soon to be sister-in-law," she explained. "She's dating my husband's brother. We're all waiting with bated breath for him to pop the question already."

I liked her laugh. It was throaty, like Janis Joplin, but a welcoming kind of laugh, like everyone in the room could be in on the joke.

"Alright, I'm going to start recording," Bear said, smiling a soft smile that I found oddly soothing. "There's no need to be nervous. We'll just carry on a totally normal conversation as if these gigantic black mics weren't obstructing our view."

I nodded. "Got it."

He counted down from five with his fingers.

"*Welcome back to the Bear and Raven show, making your mornings more* bearable. *I am Bear Tucker. With me is Raven. The two of us were sitting here having a chat about that segment we did a few weeks ago…How to Flirt. Remember our friend, Harlow? Well, she is back to give us an update about her fantastic trip to the*

*Aria Resort and Casino and give us some updates of the crazy things
that happened while she was there."*

"I hear you've become quite the card shark?" Raven asked,
turning her chair toward me.

"It was the craziest thing," I told her. "I took my sister with
me because she really needed a vacation. She's an E.R. nurse and
has been going through her own share of heartbreak."

"That's really nice of you," Bear said. "Is she older or
younger?"

"Older. By eighteen months."

"So you're at the hotel and stumble into a poker tournament,
I hear?"

"Totally by accident," I agree. "I'm not even much of a
gambler—but I had a bout of dumb luck and a dealer suggested a
tournament and suddenly there I am, playing in this thing, and
doing kind of well, thanks to my friend, Cash."

"Oh...did you hear that, Bear?"

"You mean how her voice changed when she said his name?
Yep, I caught that."

"Come on, give us the goods." Raven cajoled, "That blush has
my Spidey senses going haywire."

"I met a man when I was there. And...well, he in a
roundabout way, kind of taught me how to flirt. And with those
skills and paying really good attention to other people at the table,
I somehow made it to the winner's circle."

"Okay. Enough about winning in poker. I want to hear more
about the guy and this flirting thing." Bear pursued like a dog
with a bone.

"Oh, gosh. It's hard to make it make sense." I tried to find the
right words. But it hurt. It hurt like hell to think about him. To
speak his name. To recount all of the ways that he forced me to
look at myself and helped me recognize I was someone.

"Meeting Cash, I got to see myself entirely through someone
else's eyes. And I really liked who I was. In fact, I fell in love with
myself in Las Vegas. All thanks to Cash. He showed me a different

version of myself, not clouded by my own ingrained beliefs about my shortcomings. It was freeing in the best way, and I'll never be able to repay him for that."

I realized I was crying. Thankfully, not an ugly sobbing kind of thing, but they choked me and rolled down my cheeks unhindered. All of his complimentary words. Everything he said to me that I thought had been raindrops in the ocean were, in fact, little pebbles against a house of glass. His attention, his overt attraction, fed the flower of my soul. He held my jaw, made me look in the mirror, and forced me to find all of the beauty that made me, *me*. That was his gift. And it was better than the Louis Vuitton bag, or the ten grand to help Lennox.

"Well, don't leave us hanging!" Raven cut through my musings. "What happened with Mr. Cash?"

I could only shrug my shoulders and croak a response. "I don't know. I guess we're just a *What Happens in Vegas* kind of thing."

"I don't know, Raven. I think you and I have seen too many of these kismet-y kinds of stories to believe this is the end."

"I'm with you, Bear." She took my hand and squeezed it as they continued to banter. "I don't think this is the last you'll hear from Mr. Cash. And if anything develops on the horizon, I want to be the first to know about it."

CASH

After I left Vegas and made sure that Harlow got out of Vegas safe and sound, I turned in my phone and got a new number. I wanted to distance myself forever from anything poker related, and definitely wanted no connection to Dino. Especially after I pulled a totally legal and within the regulation of WSOP—switcheroo on him.

He told me to win, after all. He said that he knew I could beat her without even trying. And I did... win anyway. She put up a good fight. He never said that in winning I needed to collect on the pot. He assumed I would, but the devil is in the details, isn't it. I hoped he was very happy with his Baccarat trophy, and the four hundred points gained to earn a seat back into the WSOP if I wanted it. Which I didn't.

I went to my parents' house in Chicago from Vegas. At least until I could figure out what my next move was. It was weird, living back at home. But at the same time, it gave my mom and I the opportunity to have long, lingering conversations on our front porch. A lot of them centered around my feelings of worthlessness, especially tied to being at fault for Beckett nearly drowning. She directed me to a fantastic trauma therapist that she saw when we were kids, just after the incident. And gifted me with the forgiveness she said I never needed. That I was just an eight-year-old boy, and no one ever expected me to be my brother's keeper. She blamed herself. Had our whole lives and spent years trying to ensure that nothing like that ever happened again.

In therapy, I discovered how that incident influenced my feelings about myself and my importance in the family dynamic as we grew up. We were working on changing that.

I missed Harlow. But, I wanted to untangle some of my shit before reaching back out to her. Before reconnecting, I wanted to sort through some of my own issues of self-worth.

I'd waited an entire month. Despite still having access to my old phone, and seeing her hopeful texts, I waited. I waited until one day she came up in therapy and my doctor pointed out that I was waiting for a perfect time that would never come. Because life was messy and complicated. It was as I drove home from that appointment, I heard her sad, pinched voice fighting back tears on a morning radio show.

"Meeting Cash, I got to see myself entirely through someone else's eyes. And I really liked who I was. In fact, I fell in love with myself in Las Vegas. All thanks to Cash."

The irony of it all was that I saw myself through *her* eyes. She showed me a version of *myself* that I felt proud of. The kind of person who had a future and possibilities that existed outside of smoke-filled casinos and dingy hotel rooms.

Dear Bear + Raven,

Last week, you interviewed a woman by the name of Harlow about her trip to Las Vegas. I'm wondering if I could enlist your help. You see, just as she found transformation in our meeting, I too discovered that Harlow brought a peace to my soul I never realized needed settling until I met her. I'm hoping that you might do me a huge favor and help arrange a way for me to apologize to her.

Cash Murray

"Raven, you'll never guess who emailed me last night!"

"It's Monday morning, Bear. Can you just tell me without all of the theatrics?"

"Mmm, not quite. You see, they emailed me asking me for help. And I know that this is one person you will be over the moon to offer your assistance to."

"Okay, so if I'm being cloak and daggered...who's doing the assisting?"

"Ahh, right on time! Thank you for joining us, mystery guest who is arriving in our studios and taking a seat. Would you like to tell Raven here, who you are?"

"Cash Murray."

"Why does that name sound so familiar, Bear...omigod. CASH MURRAY! Vegas!"

"Our friend here has a whole lot to apologize for, it turns out. And you know that here at the Bear and Raven Show, we excel at grand gestures and apologetic gestures."

"Where's my husband? Penn isn't in on this, is he? I know what happens when the two of you have gestures of apology. This poor guy will be crying every time he pees for six months."

"Raven, you're scaring him. She's talking about a piercing, Cash. We tend to take our apologies a bit to the extreme here...tattoos or Prince Alberts."

"Or Apadravyas"

"Not helping, Raven."

"I just wanted to be accurate. Because you know if Penn thinks anyone in Chicago assumes he went with the Prince Albert, he'll be whining for weeks telling me how much worse it is to get an Apadravya than it is to get a Prince Albert."

"Anyway, Cash...now that you're mic'd up, what is it that you'd like to say?"

"Harlow, if you're listening, I want you to know that I heard you. I heard everything you said, and everything you didn't say. I heard how you said it, and the pinch in your voice. I hope our month apart has at least brought a bit of clarity, and you know that I did what I did to keep you safe. I never lied about my attraction to you, my belief in your beauty, your charm, and your warrior spirit. I looked up the meaning of your name, incidentally, and that's what you are. A warrior. Strong, battle ready. Willing to take up arms for an altruistic cause. That's what you did. You saw your sister hurting, and you immediately sought the route to alleviate that pain. And I admire the hell out of you for it. That's all I wanted to say, really. I'm sorry for everything, but especially for you ever doubting that every time I looked at you, I saw nothing but a magnificent woman who was charming, incredibly sexy, and a hell of a card shark."

I didn't know what to say. What words or combination of *I'm sorrys* would unlock the chamber to her heart. I just needed *her*. Wanted to have her with me, to see what a future together looked like.

"Listen, Cash, I'm a romantic." Raven removed her headphones and turned her chair toward me. "Harlow works two blocks north on Lasalle. At the Lyric. She's a stage manager, so my guess is she isn't there first thing in the morning, but I'd suggest a follow up."

I would do exactly that.

CHAPTER 27

Harlow

pulled into the employee lot at work, ready for yet another day of dress rehearsals. I felt like a zombie. Numb, emotionless, just going through the motions.

Standing by the backstage door was a familiar figure with his hands in his pockets, and a pair of mirrored sunglasses, a soft smile on his lips.

I refused to acknowledge my dumb heart surging to life when I saw him.

"How long have you been here?" I asked, meeting him at the third step.

"Since seven thirty this morning." He chuckled. "I paid a visit to the Bear and Raven show first. Raven sent me this way."

It felt awkward standing there. I didn't know what to say. *Hey, the ten grand was great. Sorry you risked getting killed by a mobster and I told you, you made me sick.*

"I've thought about you a lot." I admitted. "I know now, the way it went down with Lennox. I know she was wrong. You weren't using me. Or pretending."

"I know I'm a poker player, which by and large requires a *bit* of acting, but my attraction to you, my interest, infatuation, whatever word you want to use for me not being able to stop thinking about you and wondering if you're okay...that? I couldn't fake that," he said, pushing his sunglasses on his head so I could see the earnest entreaty in his eyes.

"I know," I repeated. "I figured it out on the plane ride home. I texted...I never heard back, so I just assumed that we were just a fling."

"Harlow, I promise, if you forgive me, if you give me a chance to date you, and get to know me while I get to know you...you'll figure out real fast that I would never in a million years be able to reduce what we had to just a fling. I feel like the best version of myself when I'm with you. And I really like that guy. This month away from you, Harlow, it made me realize how one-color my life was before meeting you. You make me want to find all the ways I can bring color back into my life. Because, Hollywood, you deserve nothing but the brightest rainbow."

EPILOGUE

Harlow

ix Months Later

"Ms. Prince, if you don't get a move on, my brother will be getting married without his best man."

The last six months with Cash had been nothing short of euphoric. He officially moved to Chicago to be both closer to me and his parents. While Beckett felt a bit slighted that Cash wouldn't be joining him on the west coast, he was excited for our future together, and made us promise to come together at least once a year for some kind of sibling and significant others holiday weekend.

"Well, Mr. Murray...if it wasn't for you getting my lingerie all tangled when you bent me over that occasional chair, I wouldn't have any trouble getting back into my dress. Be sure to let your brother know when you're making excuses and apologies as you rush down the aisle, that the reason you're walking in *after* the bride is because you couldn't keep it in your pants for a few hours."

"Hollywood, if it was up to me, we'd stay naked in bed twenty- four hours a day, seven days a week, so I'd have access to you whenever I wanted. In fact, there will come a point in time when jewelry is given with a question, and we do like Lane and

Beckett are about to... and after that is a step that involves a lot of nudity and absolutely no barriers. That is what I'm looking forward to. I will take an entire hiatus from the show however many months you'll let me keep you naked in bed, and happily report for duty morning, noon, and night."

After moving to Chicago, Bear and Raven introduced Cash to their boss, Genevieve Hursch. She owned the satellite radio company that housed the Bear and Raven Show. Given the popularity of Texas Hold Em, she'd offered Cash his own show, talking all things poker. It aired once a week, every Friday night. Surprisingly, he had quite the following. Though I knew how good he was, so maybe it didn't come as quite a surprise.

I tried not to get flutters in my belly every time he talked about getting married and having babies. Though, being Mrs. Cash Murray sounded like the perfect icing to our cake. At one time, I desperately lacked the confidence to flirt for a radio station contest even jokingly, and now, thanks to Cash Murray, the tiny seeds of confidence he'd helped sow had blossomed into an entire forest that was nurtured and watered under his gentle guidance.

"Hollywood, it isn't fair that you show up the bride."

He pulled me into his chest, taking a lazy journey across my mouth.

"Cash, this is exactly how we ended up being late in the first place."

I'd once told Raven that Cash didn't just fill me with compliments and suddenly, I overflowed with self-confidence. He held up a mirror and encouraged me to love the version of myself that he saw.

"I love you, Cash Cole Murray."

I laced my fingers through his as we walked where his family gathered. He grazed his lips across my knuckles, smiling that eye crinkling smile that told me I'd touched him all the way down in his soft parts.

"Thank you for showing me how to love myself."

"I'll spend every day of the rest of my life reminding you just how easy it is to love you."

Despite not knowing *how* to flirt, my champ never missed an opportunity to shower me in diamonds, make me flush, and set me straight whenever that monster of self-doubt tried to club me with recrimination. Whether fate or luck, Cash Cole Murray was the king of my heart.

WILLOW'S MEA CULPA

For those who have read me before, you know that I use my mea culpa to admit/acknowledge/accept all of the shit that I took serious creative license on in my book. As a reminder this is a literal last minute brain dump thrown into the back of the book just before I hit publish—so there's probably going to be typos. No one sees this but me.

1. I have no idea how Heathers got incorporated into this book. Maybe because Atlantic City was super popular in the eighties? Maybe because Stranger Things just ended and Winona Rider was on my mind. Actually I think I even dropped a Beatlejuice reference in here so it had to be Winona on my mind haha. Anyhow. I kind of dig it. I had the biggest crush on Christian Slater in high school (MY vanity behooves me to clarify that I went to high school in the **very late nineties**... nowhere near the eighties BUT those movies were cult classics by the time I hit high school). Mmm I'd order up a Judd Nelson/Christian Slater sandwich any day of the week.

2.When I started plotting this book, I honestly had no idea WSOP was even still a thing. I'd asked for help on Facebook first and the general opinion had been that World Series of Poker had run its course and didn't operate anymore. Until, I did some internet research while I wrote this only to discover that there actually was a WSOP tournament IN Las Vegas OVER fourth of July weekend. Well, shit. That was not intentional. So if you're like yeah it was at the wrong hotel, mea culpa I had zero intention of even having anything similar to an actual tournament occurring at the same time.

Also, other than playing Texas Hold'Em with relatives at the holidays I don't have experience at an actual poker table. Unlike Harlow, I've never had the balls to sit down and randomly start playing with strangers that won't kindly remind me when I'm the little blind the big blind or I'm on the button.

The structure of **this** game is actually a hybrid of two different styles of play so if you're a poker enthusiast saying "Willow you ain't right." I know. Mea Culpa.

The #SIROTI I read about predatory backers is actually true. There's a lot of shady people in Vegas trying to prey on trusting people who don't know much about sponsorships. I fell down a deep deep research hole on subreddit after subreddit about ridiculous amounts of money that people still owed to their supposed "backers"--- there's another word for them – its not called a backer. It's someone who fronts the buy-ins for the big tournaments in exchange for a share of the players winnings, except its an upside down pyramid that many lower tier inexperienced players never find a way to win themselves out of. So while "Dino" isn't real, he's an amalgamation of the things people in that subreddit discussed.

3. One of my many jobs as a marketer was for a casino. I know way more about gambling laws and the riverboat gambling act of 1990... but I digress. In Illinois, where I lived prior to moving to eternal summer, you could only have boats floating on the water. And one hour a day, the casino has to "close" in order to roll its books to the next day. I have no idea how they do this in Vegas or if they even have to be technically closed for a period of time. But I remember watching all of the gamblers, the ones that had legitimate problems trying to stay away from the casino, waiting

desperately...pacing the floor, watching the clock until the gates raised again and they could get back to their table because they were convinced if the casino staff wouldn't have made them get up from their table/slot machine/ video poker terminal they would have hit it big.

It was really hard to watch to be honest. I didn't work in Casino Marketing for very long (one very long summer concert season and the winter and I was gone before the next summer concert season started). But...it was those (mostly men) who seeped desperation from their pores that I imagined would be playing with Cash and Harlow in this level of tournament. The kind that don't have the glamor of the big wins.

4. There's a lot of discussion lately on BookTok surrounding the need for trigger warnings and discussions of potential triggers. Just this morning I saw a review excoriating a plus size writer for not including a trigger warning for harmful/hurtful language. I haven't read the book she discussed so I have no idea how harmful or hurtful the language was.

I've also been heavy literally my whole life... like my mom shipped me off to fat camp at *nine* (I think I turned 10 the October after I came back... the details are fuzzy. Though my mom insists to this day that I would call her crying about a mean girl named Monica that attended camp with me...and if you've ever read Monica Lewinsky's tell-all book she and I attended the same fat camp. Though I am 100% certain I never called home complaining about a Monica. I still can vividly picture the girls in my dorm and none of them looked like her). Anyway, I digress, again.

My litmus for what is potentially triggering might not be the same as someone younger. If I had a dollar for every time someone has called me a fat bitch I'd be a millionaire. So I don't personally feel like it's that triggering of a phrase but 🤐🤷 Apologies if you were triggered by a character's fat phobia.

I was attempting to show the contrast between surrounding oneself with people who love you just because you're you and people who that's all they see. And then people in-between like Harlow's sister.

Lennox's story is coning up in January. And many of you might be on the hate train because she's kind of an asshole—but you'll learn why she is in King of the Cul De Sac (its one of the few books I have that is set at a $0.99 preorder)

Coming next month is Presley's story. I have to say— the Murray Brothers and the King Siblings have been the kismety-est kismet I've experienced yet in my books. And y'all should know by now how much I gobble that shit up like hot fudge covered ice cream. But you'll have to wait until Presley's story for all the kismet goodness because I can't tell the story without giving away literally the entire book (and potentially Lennox's too.).

5. I have zero beef with Vegas. It's been a spell since I've been there— my BIL is celebrating his 40th there in December so I'll be heading there soon...but just because *Cash* as a gambler who got fucked over in Vegas hates Vegas... don't send the convention and visitors bureau after me. Haha. Same goes for Louis Vuitton.

I get into these weird patterns where all I want to do is watch documentaries, and I remember watching a string of them on Las Vegas from the gangsters, to old Vegas, to how new Vegas is a gigantic machine owned by all of like 2 corporations. I figured someone as disenfranchised by Vegas as Cash is... would definitely know these weird facts about how Vegas just feeds into itself in this unending machine.

6. I had no idea that the Fox Concept restaurants had expanded into Las Vegas. The Henry is one of my absolute favorite restaurants here in eternal summer and to see they have one across the street from the Aria where my peeps were supposedly staying #KISMET

7. I didn't link all of the Love on the Air books in the end of this. But Bear and Raven are part of the Love on the Air series. If you want to read about them... you can start with *Screwg'd* .

I have a book about Penn's (Raven's husband) brother, Bryce, that will release at the end of this month (Date and Switch...now linked at the back of this book) —releasing 10/3 that brings the morning show group back into the forefront of story telling again — and I literally can't wait to release that book. It's been sitting on my editors proverbial desk since January and I *finally* have it back and ready to publish.

I'm obsessed with Date and Switch (Bryce's story). I can't wait for you all to have it in your hands.

Alright, I say every time "I can't believe I had this much to say" like suddenly Im surprised that, as a writer, I could be so verbose 😄 😐 🤦

Anyhow, as always thank you to the Unicorn Squad and to Andi Lynne. You all have the most special places in my heart. Thank you for showing me what true friendship looks like. I love you each to infinity.

PAY A VISIT TO WILLOW'S WORLDS!

<u>Love on the Air Series</u>

<u>Screwg'd</u> (Bear & Marley)

<u>Bed of Roses</u> (Raven & Penn)

<u>Independence Bae</u> (Bear & Marley, Raven & Penn and some old friends from Dirty Little Secret & Secrets of the Heart)

<u>The Miller Sisters (Love on the Air Spinoff)</u>

<u>Date & Switch</u> (Sera Miller & Bryce Ellis (Penn's Brother)

<u>Rental Clause</u> (Felicity Miller & Klaus Baer)

Under a Starless Sky (Date & Switch Spin Off) – Appeared in Christmas Anthology will release soon

<u>Enemies in Ernest</u> (Acacia & Edwin (Klaus' Cousin)

Salve (Rex Miller & Regina Cole - Felicity & Sera's brother) Coming soon!

<u>The Murray Brothers</u>

<u>Thirst Trap</u> (Beckett & Lane)

<u>Flirt Like a Champ</u> (Cash Murray & Harlow Prince)

<u>Secret Santa</u> (Priscilla King & Presley Murray)

Harris' Story coming soon

<u>King of the Cul De Sac</u> -*Murray Brothers Spin Off*- (Lennox Shaw & Jesse King) Harlow's Sister & Priscilla's Brother

<u>The Barren Hill Series</u>

<u>Beard on Tap</u> (Finn & Gemini)

<u>Codename: Dustoff</u> (Emmett & Amelia)

<u>Whiskey Business</u> - *A Barren Hill Spinoff*- (Jasper & Remle)

A Whole New World (*A Whiskey Business Spinoff*, Coming soon)

The Jones Brothers (Coming Soon!)

Capivate Me (Sterling Cooper Jones)

Titillate Me   (Sullivan Carter Jones)

Extracurricular Academics

Booking Dr. Wrong (Dr. Patrick Ryan & Tabitha Spence)

Witch Please (Dr. Sebastian Doyle & Dr. Imogen Pilar)

Missed Connections (Dr. Phoebe Wagner & Anders Larcohette)

The Royals - An Extracurricular Academics Spin Off

Mile High Monarch (A Missed Connections Spin Off)

The Expireship (A Mile High Monarch Spin Off) Coming Soon!

Deck Pic (Sawyer & Wren)

Romantic Suspense

I Will Always Find You & Found (The Jefe Duet)

Contemporary New Adult

Dirty Little Secret

Secrets of the Heart

MEET PRESLEY MURRAY & PRISCILLA KING

Presley

I can't go anywhere without someone asking if I'm the brother of *the* Beckett Murray. Yes, I am. The middle brother. Also, a swimmer who was never good enough to make the Olympic cut. The new job in Texas couldn't have come at a better time. Finally, I'll be able to make my mark on the swimming world as a coach for a Big 12 University.

My landlord asks me to take part in some kind of auction I have zero time to take part in, and just to get her to leave me alone, I agree to take part in her Secret Santa exchange among the residents of Fitzpatrick Place. The woman I get? A sinfully curvy woman named Priscilla who owns a kitschy little diner on the edge of town. I'll play along for the week of gift-giving and merriment, but I need to show the university that while I'm not my brother, I'm equally skilled in the pool. I can't afford any distractions. So why can't I stop thinking of her smile, the way she sings along to the jukebox when she thinks no one is paying attention, or how sexy she looks in those unassuming fifties dresses?

Priscilla

I've lived in Fitzpatrick Place ever since I moved back home five years ago. Had it been risky overhauling my mom's greasy spoon to a fifties-inspired, Elvis-themed diner? Maybe. But, from the moment I stepped into my *blue suede shoes* five years ago, I'd yet to slow down.

Fitzy exhausted herself trying to play matchmaker for me. I just didn't have time. That diner was my whole life. I reluctantly agreed to be part of the building's Secret Santa gift exchange, getting some new guy in D3 who was practically a ghost. He would get some cute gifts from me because I had no time to introduce new people to the neighborhood or entertain total strangers. I'd do my best at holiday cheer—but it would be the bare minimum.

One day he plays messenger for my own Secret Santa, and suddenly I see him everywhere: the bookstore, the elevator, and call me crazy, but it feels like he's finding any excuse to come to the diner.

Now he's *always on my mind,* and I can't *just pretend* that I'm not *all shook up* every time he looks at me with those deep blue eyes and uneven smile. I guess *it's now or never,* especially since I'm *lonesome tonight.* Hopefully, putting myself out there won't land me in the *heartbreak hotel*.

Secret Santa is a curvy heroine, matchmaker, holiday romance that is guaranteed safe with no cheating and no cliffhangers. Why not spend some time at Fitzpatrick Place?

Available for Pre Order

MEET LENNOX SHAW & JESSE KING

He reported her to the HOA and now he's about to learn you don't cross Lennox Shaw. But when an emergency pops up and his help is her only option, she'll soon realize the "Little Napoleon," isn't afraid of a skirmish or two.

MEET BECKETT MURRAY & LACHLAN DEVEREAUX

Lachlan Devereaux had exactly two hundred and eighteen days remaining to hit the Forbes 30 Under 30 list. With a new product line ready to launch and her steering the marketing team, she was certain this was the success she needed to receive the venerated recognition. What she hadn't expected is what happened in Vegas not to stay in Vegas. Enter Beckett Murray—stage left.

Beckett Murray just wanted to be taken seriously for once. His bad-boy days were behind him, and he wanted everyone—including the Olympic swimming team—to realize he had grown up and wasn't still that punk kid anymore. He bought an organic beverage company to prove to everyone he was solid, in pursuit of adult goals, and not the partying playboy they all thought he was. Until he came face to face with his Las Vegas one-night stand. He couldn't afford a scandal right now—but he hadn't stopped thinking about that amazing night five months ago.

When old friends become adversaries, and the company's success is put in jeopardy, their thirst for each other could just be their recipe for success.

Grab it Today!

ABOUT THE AUTHOR

willowwriting.com